# The Laughing Elf

Also published by Nodens Books:

*Above Ker-Is and Other Stories*, by Evangeline Walton

*Lady Stanhope's Manuscript and Other Stories*, by Dale Nelson

# The Laughing Elf

by

## Ronald MacDonald

*"Risus harmonia discordantium."*

Nodens Books

2017

*The Laughing Elf*

First published by Nodens Books, 2017
This edition copyright © Nodens Books, L.L.C.
Cover art by Roy Meldrum
ISBN 9781976491627
Printed in the United States of America
First edition: October 2017

Nodens Books
PO Box 493
Marcellus, MI 49067

www.nodensbooks.com

TO
ROY M. RIDLEY
FOR THE KINDNESS THAT HAS BEEN AND IS

# Contents

# The Laughing Elf

# I.

## The Laughing

Once upon a time, when men knew less and fairies little more than now, there was an elf that was unhappy. No fairy loved him, none played with him twice, and few even made as if they saw him passing by.

Fairyland being the only country that he knew, though little of it, he could not have told you where he was, nor who he was, nor why he was. And the *who* was the doubt which most troubled him: if he could but know that, he thought, he might perhaps discover his *what-for-ness*.

Had you and I then seen his little crumpled face with its funny, sharp ears, we should not have laughed; and when in a pool of some clear rivulet, he would examine it himself, he could not smile; for the frown he saw reflected was of puckered perplexity, showing neither judgment nor disgust.

And from this contemplation he would turn always to renew his elfish quest of he knew not what.

Sometimes, however, awaking from dreams he could not remember, this anxious elf would be filled for a while with belief that discovery had been very near; so it came about that a little thing in him, which he did not yet know for hope, tempted him often and yet more often to break his wandering search by curling himself down to sleep in any place which he fitted softly enough; and one morning, in early dawn, he awoke to find.

He had lain down at the edge of a dark wood of pine-trees which stood upon the very border of fairyland; and he opened his crinkled eyelids to peer out over the rim of the small, turf-padded hollow which had made his bed.

Towards him, from the gentle bands of grey light, brooding over the birth-place of the sun, came Sorrow, the cloud of her black garment now swinging out soft and thin, and again, with her slackening approach, closing about her, dark and heavy to the feet.

Her name the elf did not know; but when he was so near that he could see her eyes, his little heart fell and sank away from him until it seemed melting into the earth.

Never seeing the small face which stared at her from below, Sorrow gazed ever far above it towards the dark wall of the pine-wood, until the elf must turn about to know, even though he feared, what it was that she saw or waited to see.

Out of the wood, dim at first, but soon sure and splendid, came Joy. At sight of the dark form which he did not know, his pace was quickened until Sorrow and he looked each into the other's eyes.

Softly and secretly our elf sat himself down upon the brink of his hollow, with his back toward the growing light, and looked up into the strange faces of this pair that met in the dawn. For his heart had come back to him out of the ground, so that never again should he be afraid.

And for all that he did not know who they were, he yet said within himself, looking from the one countenance to the other:

"It is a marvel: neither knoweth the other, but neither could know himself if the other were not! Are they enemies, or do they belong?"

Deeper and deeper above him gazed the two pairs of eyes. The two heads were bent together, as if across some barrier between their bodies; and our elf, looking downward from those two faces which had filled him with wonder, saw for the first time, standing between Sorrow and Joy, a little white fellow whose golden head, shining before there was ever a ray from the sun to gild it, was but breast high to the pair.

When they kissed above him, this naked stranger touched them with a hand apiece, and they looked down upon him, stepping apart.

"Who art thou?" asked Sorrow, bending over, so that some little wind swept a fold of her robe about him. And the elf saw how those slender white limbs shone through the blackness.

Then, before Sorrow had her answer,

"Who art thou, shining there?" asked Joy.

With his right hand the little fellow touched Sorrow upon the arm.

"I am your his-ness," he said, bending his eyes upon Joy.

"For you," he said, as his left hand touched Joy's arm, "I am your her-ness."

Then those two looked the more each at the other, asking, as with one voice, of him they no longer regarded,

"But thou—thou thyself—who art thou?"

Then the elf saw that the loose billow of Sorrow's robe fell back, so that the whiteness of him whose name they sought shone, with the nearing sun, brighter even than before.

"I am not myself a *me*," he answered. "But, when I am grown up, I am going to be the me-ness and the you-ness of all the world."

The light grew, sending now upward spears to the soft grey clouds. So the elf saw the tears which ran down the three faces of his worship, and above them such a shining of the eyes which shed them as made him cast down his own from the brightness; so that he saw a tiny, yellow-cupped flower at his knee, even now about opening its night-tightened lips.

10

"Those tears," he thought, "are wasted, if they do not mingle," and, plucking the flower for a cup, he made shift to catch with it one shining drop from each passion.

Then it was that the sun shot along the earth his first level ray, piercing grass-blades and tight heather-bells with all their wet jewelry of quivering diamonds. And the elf turned his back upon the three that wept, and lifted his slender-stemmed, yellow-bowled goblet into the sunbeam.

Through cup and liquor shone the light, and he saw a colour which you and I believe in, although we have not seen it ever in prism nor in dewdrop—saw it, and never saw again, but always.

So he lifted his cup and drank what it held, knowing a savour which has not faded even to this day

He drank and fell asleep in his grass-lined pocket of the hillside. Sleeping, he dreamed of the heart of things, and, when he awoke, remembered how one was nothing, and another was nothing, and how that a third could not alone exist; and how yet the three were all things and everybody.

So well did he see into this clear mystery, knowing all its ins and outs better than the most, industrious of school-girls her tables of multiplication, that he leapt to his feet and began running down the hill in the moonlight, saying in his quick-beating heart:

"I will go and tell them—tell them—tell everybody!"

He ran until he came to a wide green place, in a village of men and houses asleep.

In the middle of the green he stood panting, and scratching his hot, pointed ears in perplexity.

He must tell them of the three nothings that were everything; of the new colour; and of the white limbs of that little fellow, which shone through the smoky black garment that was not his. But how tell?

How to tell the best tale that ever there was, to ears shut in sleep—and a tale for which, after all, the words were not yet fashioned?

A strange passion panted in his breast and throbbed in his throat.

"A tale which will not be told; a tale which has no words; a tale for ears which cannot listen and for heads that do not wish to know! A tale which must get out—a tale that will not stay at home!"

So ran his thought, while a sort of tickling came to the throbbing in his throat. This was absurd; and, since he knew no such word, yet felt its very inmost meaning, he fell sitting to the grass, flung back his head, and sent out over the world the first laughing it ever knew: for he had found, without knowing he had found it, the language for telling at least the beginning of the story which he had seen.

Before his last slumber he had seen the secret of the likenesses, the unlikenesses, and all the degrees of all the differences which are among all

11

men and all things. The draught from the yellow cup had made him drunk with love of the great picture, and when he awoke, that new colour which is not found even in the rainbow was his for everywhere and always.

So he lifted his voice to tell it all to all the world, and many folk of that village heard the new language of laughter.

## II

## Lubber Long Legs

Once upon the same time—a few months, maybe, before ever the Elf laughed—there came to dwell in a house by the green place whence the laugh should arise thereafter in the moonlight, a couple that were newly husband and wife.

These two, after a certain while lived together; because of their love to each other, which was greater than between most wedded couples before the laughing came to the village, they began to find that all was not well with them: for there would come at times a frost, as it seemed, of failure in the two passions which should have grown to one love; each of the pair finding the other to be a country of which the coasts and the great central city were well known; but between the few roads from sea to capital lay vast spaces untravelled and unmapped.

Now one, now the other would wander down a by-road, which would dwindle to a half-beaten foot-track, or stop dead at some river-bank, or ravine of the hills; and then the trouble that there was to find the way back without stumblings, wounding and tears!

The woman, having yet no child, would lose her way more often in the island of her exploration than the man in his: for his day's work was in the fields, or on the hillside, or among the real trees, while hers was always in the same paddock and barn and cottage.

So one day, after she had lost herself and he had found her again, he fetched her home a plaything.

He carried it into the barn and laid it upon thick straw in the most sheltered corner. For, although its legs were many and very long, they could not yet uphold the short body and the heavy, foolish head which belonged to them.

Looking down upon this helplessness, the young wife had pity on the creature—and a little shuddering of horror also, for the strangeness of its shape. The Elf being not yet come to her village, she did not know how to make these two feelings into one; but, being a kind woman, she pushed the horror away from her, and laid her hand upon the melancholy head to stroke it.

" 'Tis a small horse," she said, "but I think the shape is wrong."

A few months later she would have known it for and called it a *horse-baby*; but the likenesses and the differences had not yet begun their shouting to each other.

"Hast never seen a mare's foal, woman!" asked her husband. "It was born but last night, and the mother died this morning. They had no milk for it up there," he went on, explaining uneasily. " 'Twas give him to me or let him die, and I thought you'd maybe take kindly to him, feed him and handle him, until—"

His wife looked up, waiting for the words which did not come.

"Until he is strong enough to run, and graze in our paddock," he said.

She knew it was not what he had tried to say. But she nodded so that he knew she had understood him, and ran to bring warm milk for the foal.

So for many days did the woman fondle and tend that queer little beast; until, she lifting, he stood upon uncouth legs and did not fall.

And when he came to staggering a few paces unhelped to the door of the barn; next, to shuffling sadly over the short grass of the paddock; and at last, between long standings, to perilous trottings and amblings, the woman's heart grew greater with love to her foundling in measure as he needed her the less. And the man, watching, also loved the colt, for the love which the woman had to it.

Thus between them they learned and did all that is best for a young horse that is an orphan.

Now for a while this love in common opened roads and made easier travelling in those secret islands of each other's understanding. But after a greater while, light still lacking from that colour which is not even in the rainbow, they began, not knowing what they did, to love the colt against each other.

The man felt it first (and first knew it for division of love) in his desire to put out his will and blandishments against his wife's tender enticement of the colt to follow her way rather than her husband's. And in the same moment she had vision of what the man abstained himself from doing; yet never found the like thing in herself, not even while she did it.

So it was that, some hours before the Elf woke from his long sleep upon the hillside, there rose a quarrel between them.

The man, coming home at sundown, had scarce swallowed a mouthful of his supper before he asked, how was the colt?

"He shall drink his milk with us," answered the wife. "And you shall see how fine he grows—and his coat smoother and softer every day that goes by."

In happiest mood she ran to the safe stall they had built for their darling, against the barn's end; but returned too soon, with face pale and lips a-tremble.

14

"He is gone," she whispered.

The man rose in such haste of anger that his chair was overset, falling noisily.

"Did I not bid you fit the bar to his crib every night, now that he ambles so swift, and is come to such strength?" he asked.

Then, because it was as he had said, the woman also was angry.

In the paddock they found nothing but a gap in the fence which divided it from a field of barley yet green.

"If he stay there an hour and eat," said the man, "he will die."

Divers ways among the corn they went, but had no fruit of all their calling.

Meeting again at the broken panel of the fence, they fell to wrangling. Her fault angered them both, until the woman, lest she should weep under the eyes of her accuser, ran from him and flung herself down, face to turf, behind a clump of willows which grew beside the brook that cut the lower corner of the paddock. And there, as her sobbing and sighing broke strongly from her, she did not hear the soft, quick drumming of the unshod hoofs which her grief had sent trotting out from the mist-wrapped willows.

But the man saw his wife's lost plaything coming up the field to him, moving ever slower as he approached, until at last he stood, head up and snuffing the wind; whereby the man knew that the little beast had taken his first taste of freedom.

"He runs already swifter, maybe, than I. But 'tis an animal," said the man to himself, "curious as a magpie."

And so cast himself full length upon the grass.

Whereupon the young horse flung his head upward and sidewise, so that his long forelock streamed for a moment in the breeze which already was shifting the mist from the hollow where he had lurked among the willows.

There was one man only that he knew—perhaps two others that he had seen; but none of them to fall and lie still as a tree-log.

With clumsy delicacy he made a few steps towards his master and smelt the wind again; then came a little nearer still.

The fallen man did not stir, and the colt stood like an image cast of bronze.

With a slit of one eye open, the man whistled three notes of a little tune; upon which the colt started aside, and wheeled, looking round him; then stood once more.

It was thus that the woman saw him again. For the sound of her own grief had died away, and her foundling's snorts of doubt came down the wind to her, so that she arose and crept softly between the willow-trees and saw him stiff against the line of the sky in the moonlight. Till he

15

should move, she dared not. But when he trotted three paces of each leg towards his fallen master, she travelled many yards more, running wondrous soft while his little thudding footsteps were sounding in his own silly ears.

Twice more the colt thus approached what he could not understand, and twice the woman gained ground upon him. So that, when he stood at last, snuffing with trembling velvet lips all up his master's body from knee to chin, she was near enough to know his curiosity, and for a moment which was like a knife's stab, to share his misgiving.

But a hand that she knew, between the colt's brown neck and the moonlight shining white as until now she had never seen it, crept up and up till its fingers made a tight handful of the dancing forelock.

Then the man rose, lifting himself partly by that tuft of hair, so that you might have seen the little beast's overlong forelegs to tremble at the knees with the weight of a moment.

No sooner, however, was his master erect, than the colt rubbed his nose in the man's breast and was content.

But the woman, now that the beast was plainly safe, and her husband neither overcome as she had feared, by grief nor by sickness, lost all joy in this security. For it was whelmed at once in a passionate resentment which told her that each of these loved the other better than either her.

Could she have hidden herself, she would have fled once more; knowing herself still unseen, she sank to her knees, head bowed in hands—a small heap in the moonlit field.

Then it was that the Elf laughed.

The woman, behind eyelids and covering hands, saw herself a child again, that watched a stream of green and golden bubbles rising; whereof each bubble as it broke sprinkled the world with froth of heart's ease and love.

So she rose, opening her eyes, and heard, from the village-green beyond her cottage, the bubbles still rising.

There came a throb in her breast and a soft gurgle of laughing in her throat.

She saw her husband fling his arms wide and high, and heard from his mouth a long shout, rising and falling in tone and volume with the inward breath and the outward. And she saw the colt, for the first time, fling up thrice in quick iteration his hinder heels, squeaking the while; next, to trot wheeling in a circle until his first whinny died with a soft, kindly grumbling in his throat; then to stand ponderingly, before putting a fine finish to his display by leaping, back arched to a hump, all four legs together, from the ground.

As he hung a moment in the air, the hunched body seemed smaller, the head greater and the legs longer than ever.

16

She thought again of her childhood, and of animals which were children with her.

The husband came beside her, his arm round her, his soft laughter in her ears.

The colt, surprised by the jar of his four-footed return to earth, bent to his mistress a shaggy head full of questions.

"He is like—like something else," said the man.

"My father had a donkey," said the woman. "He's like a donkey on stilts!"

Laughing all the way, they took the colt home to supper.

It is not known, say the wise, whether a man or a woman was the first to laugh; but it is certain that the first joke was a woman's.

This couple soon believed that it was the finding of the colt and their falling again into love which taught them to laugh; but if you should chance to meet with the Laughing Elf, that was close friends with their eldest born, he might tell you a tale like mine.

Reaching the threshold that night, the man called the colt, which ambled lumberingly after him.

"The lubber thing that it is!" he said, and laughed once more. But the woman, smiling, said: "His poor legs are so long!"

Wherefore the man cried:

"We will call him Lubber Longlegs!"

This they did; and philosophers will tell you even now that you can never, until you have laughed at it, fashion for a living thing the name which is properly its own.

# III

## The Gates of Welcome

The moon it was which threw light about the Elf's laughing that night; but here and there were also candle-gleams, edging or dividing curtains and outlining window-frames.

One of these wounds in the earlier darkness of the night shone yellowish and dreary over the village shop—the best shop, because it was the only one.

For many years all kinds of things that the people needed had flowed out of its front door, which faced the green, almost as fast as they could be carried in, baled and boxed, from the waggons which stood in the side alley.

In the room above the shop sat, that night, the shopkeeper, between the window where the curtains did not meet each other, and a table covered with supper of which he had eaten hardly a morsel.

The room was wide, low-ceiled, well-furnished and well kept, and softly lit with candles and their light thrown up again from the white cloth.

The steel-lined oaken chest in the dark corner was full of money; the food and wine in the candle-light were good and plentiful; the carpet was soft, the wall hangings of sombre richness; but in the shopkeeper's heart was no light, no wealth, no peace, no refreshment, no beauty.

So well had he served the needs and the whimsies of his village and country-side, that he could not now, while the shop-door was open, have kept the money from pouring in. But he had come to caring so little for the people, the shop and the money, that he was in two minds this night whether or no to take down his shutters in the morning, or ever again.

There seemed to be nothing to do, because there was nothing for which the man cared: nothing, because there was nobody.

Two women, long ago, there had been: she that was not his sister had seen another man as our shopkeeper had seen her; and though his sister wept for leaving him, he could never forget that she would have wept longer and more bitterly in being left.

He was a man that, asking for the whole of it, might heartily have borne the moiety of another's sorrow; but he had not yet even conceived the sweetness there is in that pain which is the price of another's joy. He must not, however, be judged with modern stricture, for the Elf—but you shall hear.

In the village they never said that he was a bad man. Some even had called him good. But the kindest could no more than shake the head in deprecation when you should call him a hard man.

And to-night it was of his neighbours whom he loved not that our shopkeeper was thinking. Those others he forgot—the two women that had gone away, and the apprentice he had almost loved five years ago: a servant that would not stay with a good master a week after his indentures were run out!

Hard man? Why, of course they said he was hard. What is it makes the fingers callous, if not the handling of tools and the resistance of stubborn material? All that had been within his reach, he told himself, had been but tools and materials. If there had been friends for him—lovers—!

There came a sound from the roadway between the shop and the village green—footsteps and a voice; two pairs of feet, he thought, but one voice only, and few words.

He rose to look out, but at once sat down again. Why should he, for whom none cared, care for a benighted wayfarer, or a couple of late lovers?

Thinking, therefore, again only of himself, he sat with a hand shielding his eyes from even the light of the candles, and sunk so deep in self-pity that he heard no sound of the door below gently opened and closed, nor of ascending footsteps.

He did not hear even the door-latch of the very room where he sat; but, at last becoming aware that he was no longer alone in it, he lowered the covering hand from his eyes, and raised them to the face of the man that stood in the doorway.

A young man he was, tall, slender and strong, with mouth of so sweet a firmness and eyes so keen and inquisitive, that the shopkeeper did not at first know him for the apprentice who, five years ago, had left him lonelier than ever before.

"Well, master?" said the younger man; and the elder knew him at once by the voice. "I have come to see you."

"Were I your master indeed," said the old man, regarding the intruder's feet, "you might have seen me without coming so far."

"I went away," retorted the youth, "because you refused to be my master any longer."

The shopkeeper caught his breath, biting off an indignant denial. Upon his old servant, he thought, some change had come.

"Sit down," he said, with a gentle austerity; and into a silver cup he poured wine for his visitor. Already he was forgetting that life had seemed no good to him. When the traveller had drunk,

"Make that good—that I refused your service," said the shopkeeper.

"I had a good master for all the years I was with you," said the young man, "and you, sir, had a good servant; so that I knew all the things that you sell—especially the things which they bring us from the great town to sell to our country-folk—the things of beautiful iron."

The old man shrugged his shoulders and made a wry face.

"What has beauty to do with iron and steel?" he asked. "I sell for use."

"Beauty has to do with all things. You deny beauty, sir," said the young man, looking at his elder as you may see a man look for the first time at a picture, "because, having lost it in your youth, you are vexed that you do not find it again."

"It is the same for all men," said the other.

"I am older than I was, and I get more beauty every day."

"Stick to the point," said the old man, " you were to prove that I refused your service."

"I thought you had perceived my proof," said the youth. " Well, did I not say to you 'Give me half a year's bed and food while I may learn what our blacksmith can teach of his tools and materials, and I will make you things, sir—ploughs better than these ploughs, spades, rakes, cart-wheels, axles stronger and lighter than any you have ever sold?' Did I not say all that?"

The shopkeeper nodded.

"All that and more," he said.

"If you'd kept me in the shop down there, at my old toil," the young workman continued, "I should have been your slave. I offered you my best work—and that is the service of a freeman."

"Umph!" grunted the shopkeeper. "But you spoke of beauty. Your words seemed a madman's. A spade is for digging the earth—not for hanging on the wall to worship it."

"If you had not said good-bye to it thirty years ago, sir," said the craftsman, "you'd know that beauty is a dear, wild flower—grows where it pleases—where it belongs, The bits we pick out and hang painted or carved on our walls are but reminders and lesson books."

"I do good business," said the trader. "I am afraid of pretty spades and beautiful cart-wheels."

From beneath raised brows the young eyes seemed to pierce the old ones.

"Good business! Business that wearies a man until at whiles he wishes he were dead before his day?"

"How do you know?"

"I saw you before you saw me—now, when I entered. Besides," said the philosopher, "did you not say your beauty is dead?"

And getting no answer, he continued,

"So dead was it, even five years ago, that it stank, and you drove away the freed slave without ever a trial of his best work. I went home, sir, to the hills, and there should I be now, I think, but for a young woman that I love."

"Why run from her?" asked the old man. "Wait awhile, and she will save you the trouble."

"I do not run from her," said the lover. "Her father is a great person, and wealthy, and I made for him, working six months, the finest and most curious pair of gates for his house-road ever hammered out of iron. But his daughter loved the gates before they were begun, and me before I came to hanging them. And when I had done it, he sent good money to me for the working, and word that if I spoke ever with the maid again, my wages should be death. So I kissed her lips under the eye of his messenger, and—came to you once more to offer my service."

"And left the girl?"

"I have left her where she is safe—until now, at least."

"Do you come all these miles," asked the shopkeeper, "to make the old offer?" The youth nodded. "Why should you expect other than the old reply!"

"The offer is better! I have not my work to learn. Give me a forge and I will begin to-morrow."

Again there was no answer. In a lowered voice the workman spoke further.

"I looked to find you, sir, by this, of changed temper, feeling, perhaps, a lack of me—"

"I have long felt it," cried the master, interrupting the hesitation. "I would you had these swords and mattocks, ploughs and spears, axes and axles to show. If, as you say, my *beauty* be dead, I have so the keener eye for service."

Then in his mind the workman doubted whether the eye which sees not the best can see anything well; but his pity told him softly that he had but the wilfulness of a sore memory to deal with.

So he drew from his inner pocket a set of papers, wrapped close about a rundle of smoothed beechwood.

"I did not haul a waggon-load of goods with me," he said.

"If you had 'em, why not?" asked the shopkeeper. "They should get you work anywhere, if they be what you say."

"Did I not tell you, sir, my answer to the man of the gates?" said the lover. "The message was carried, make no doubt. And his riders were out after me before the sun was down—that I know."

"Know?" said the old man, beginning to remember love, and rising to pace the floor.

"I saw them. They passed the bushes where I—where I lay hiding—six men-at-arms, and very fierce fellows. But I know our hills, and here I am."

Then, after a pause, while his old master walked the room:

"No," continued the workman, "I have no cartload of all the things I have wrought, but I have drawings and pictures of some."

He laid his roll on the table, shifting plates and spoons aside, for space to spread the papers fairly upon the cloth.

Unrolling the sheets one after another, holding one down with a hand on each curling end until it made him too soon desire the next, the shopkeeper forgot that he kept a shop; forgot his age; felt his youth without memory, and, through pictures of swords, hammers, ploughs, axes, wheels, snaffles, bridoons, horse-shoes, saddle-trees, locks, griddles, spears, fire-dogs and window-bars, gloated, without knowing what gave him pleasure, over the beauty of use, until, unsuspecting, he was almost in reach of the usefulness of beauty.

When there was but one paper left, he raised his head and looked at the workman with a strange fire of eagerness in his eyes, holding out a hand for more.

"This," said the workman, unrolling the last, "will scarce please you, sir."

"Let me see," said the learner; and bent himself over the scroll for a while which seemed long to him that had traced its bold lines of savage beauty.

The gazer at last drew his breath sharply through his teeth.

"These are those iron gates," he said, "which the girl loved, and for which the girl's father has paid a price so heavy! It is strange! It is wonderful! Why it is, I do not know—but the picture draws my eye and holds it. And yet—is it beauty?"

"I think it is. There is a standpoint above the road, a furlong from the smithy where I dwelt and made those gates, whence you may see the setting sun and perhaps a reddening sky shine through them. Then you might stand still till night was come, and never take your eyes from the beauty of it."

"This," said the old man, grown strangely gentle, "I have called wonderful indeed. But it gives me no pleasure—no solace—no—no—" and so fell silent.

"Is not wonder joy of a kind?" asked the beater of iron. "But I know very well, sir, the thought in your mind. There is awe (with a red sun shining through the black latticing of it)—awe growing to fear and terror."

"And why put terror into beauty and a gateway?"

"Not any gateway—but just this gateway," said the youth. "As I make a shoe to fit every hoof that comes to me, and to suit the work it has to do, so have I suited these gates to the house and to the man that built it. To that man, sir, a gate is a thing which says No. It is there to keep you out. So I made him, of beaten, beautiful iron, through which you may see, if you stand far enough, more easily than through winter branches—I made him for a gate a dream of swords and spears and of all things which cry to that ear which we have between head and heart: 'Thou shalt not.' "

Never a man talk like this had the shopkeeper heard. The workman glanced at him and talked on.

"Not *any* gate—*that* gate," he repeated. "Yet upon that gate was I working, when I had my first thought of the gate I would one day make for myself, when I should have a house after my heart, standing well away from the high road. And once there was when almost I saw my gate."

"How was that?" asked the old man, eager to learn new things.

"The woman I told you of, sir, came upon me softly, as I sat resting by the smithy door, eyes closed. And when I felt her hand and delicate kerchief wipe the sweat from my face, I—I—well, I thought I was going to see my gate, as I see this one, which you have seen."

"Tell me of it," said the learner.

"I cannot. I do not see. I have not seen it. But my gate is a gate which says: 'Come in! Look through me and see the flowers I would not hide if I could.' A gate with oil on its hinges and kisses between its bars. But something is lacking in me—in all of us. There is a great word to be said. And then—my gate!"

Since ever he saw him standing in the doorway, love for his old servant had been trickling back into the shopkeeper's heart; but now it came in a flood. Some inkling he had, perhaps, of the holy secret which he had said was dead in him; a little came from the bright eyes, keen words and crafty pencil-work of his visitor. But his words now sprang all from his love. For in that moment he yearned over the servant come back to him as a mother over her child when she would fetch all the round moons from all the skies, for the little fat fingers to play skittles with them.

"Why, stay with me till death," he said. "You shall see your Gate of Welcome, boy—you shall see it. But first you must have the house, and before even the house must you have the woman in it. And to get the woman from her father, from behind those Gates of Refusal, I will go to the King, and tell him what manner of man you are. And I will make him see the gates, and he shall ask the daughter for you from the man who keeps her behind them. For when he has seen them, the King will want gates for his palace."

From one mouth and one pair of eyes lover and workman spoke gratitude.

"Do but find me a forge and good metal enough," he continued, when the thanks were said, "and the King may wait. Some day he shall come to me."

"But the maiden?" said the shopkeeper.

"None will find her sooner nor more easily than I," said the lover; and his eyes so shone that an old pain thrilled in the shopkeeper's heart, and he turned away abashed from the young man's gaze.

"You have not eaten, my son," he said; and would have filled a plate for him.

But the young man, excusing himself as not hungry, and beginning upon further speech of that young woman, was interrupted by the great laughing of the Elf, outside upon the village green.

In peals and waves of peals, which chased, it seemed, and overlapped each other, each billow caught and held from falling to earth by the surge of the next, the laughter arose. How long it lasted, no man knew; for, while it persisted, none had thought for time, nor eye for clock.

When it seemed at an end, having faded to a fineness of sound such that no ear could perceive where hearing ceased and memory began, the shopkeeper found himself standing in his open window, with joy in his breast, and a gurgling spasm in his throat.

He turned inward to the room, letting out a little of his own laughter for relief. But his companion, not laughing, nor in any way heeding his new master, was bent over the table, his pencil moving with wondrous speed and terrible certainty, at work upon the blank side of one of the scattered sheets.

So the master stood watching the growth beneath his eyes of the dreamed image which should soon be hammered with strength and tenderness so excellent into that marvel of ironwork long known throughout that country as The Smiling Gateway, but called in those days by the workman that dreamt and hammered it "The Gates of Welcome."

And while the loveliness of the drawing grew, there grew with it in the watcher's mind the knowledge that beauty is no mere distillation of a man's youth, but is for ever the blood of his soul's pulse.

At last the flying pencil was still, and the young man looked up at his friend.

"Did you also hear?" asked the master.

The workman smiled, his face beautiful as it had never shone before.

"Don't you see," he asked, "how some of it has stuck to my paper?"

"I think we shall not hear it again," said the old man.

"I know I shall hear it always," said the young one.

As if in answer, there came up to them, from within the house, another laughing.

"It has got inside," said the shopkeeper.

Again the workman smiled.

"Yes," he said, picking up his pencil. "Go down and find it, sir. I think 'tis in the shop;" and fell to work again on his picture.

Down to his shop, candle in hand, went the shopkeeper; and there, stretched freely on a pile of new sacks, lay a young woman sleeping. So the shopkeeper knew why his servant had said that he would be quicker than the King to find her.

The light of the candle troubled her eyelids; yet, before they were lifted, the sleeper laughed again—a laugh soft and very sweet.

"Who are you?" she asked, when her eyes gleamed blue in the candle-light.

"Your host, madam, and a friend of your lover," replied the shopkeeper. "He has sent me to fetch you. Will you come?"

She stretched a hand for his, and rose with its lift to her feet and followed him up the stair.

The door stood open, and she stole softly behind her lover bent over his work.

From behind her arm slipped round him, between shoulder and neck, and she bent her head to his.

But before lips met cheek, her eyes fell upon his work, and she forgot his close body.

She gazed in wonder till the tears came, and she sank to her knees beside him, sliding her palms down shoulder and arm to his left hand.

"Oh! Oh!" she said. "He has found it while I slept. He has found his Gates of Welcome."

And so lifted and kissed his fingers.

IV

## The Black Flames

The chief woodman of the forest lying between the village where first the Elf laughed and the hills where the ironworker hammered his first pair of gates, was a tall man of strength too great, they would say, for his own or other men's safety.

Yet was he slow of speech, untiring in work, and always as ready to help stranger as friend; nor had any in the village known him, since his manhood was reached, to use his strength unjustly. Many owed him gratitude, to forget it when its hour came: this one, for the fierce bull he had tamed; another, for his rescuing from robbers of the hills; an old woman, to save whose calf the woodman had proved himself stronger than the river in flood; and many others.

It would, nevertheless, have been hard, even in the days of his early manhood, to find one that did not in some sort fear him. A few tales, perhaps, of an outrageous anger in his boyhood, of strife between the lad and grown men or dangerous animals, wherein he had done more hurt than expected of his years, joined with his later modest bearing and silent habit to make him a man apart.

But there was one at least that feared him not at all, and grew to loving him greatly.

Down among the fat meadows which sloped to the river lived a woman that was a widow, with a good house, good fields, good cattle, and a daughter that was very good indeed, whether to look upon or to love. But the son that she had, though touching upon manhood, had given the widow woman little but sorrow for the day and fear of the morrow.

Now there came an afternoon when this son, having besought his mother to grant him a thing which she would not, found his sister in a field by the river road, fetching home the cattle. And as she would have avoided him, knowing too well why he sought her, he ran and took her by the hair and held her captive. But when still she would not consent to add her voice to his that he might prevail over their mother, he was angry, and used her so roughly that she cried out softly that he hurt her.

"And will hurt thee more, sister unsisterlike," he replied, "if thou do not obey me."

27

But, she refusing again and yet again, in the end he struck her open-handed upon the face, and the girl cried aloud in pain.

Upon her cry came the woodman, leaping the low hedge and great ditch between field and road.

The boy, stricken foolish by fear, let go his sister and shrank cringing from the vast form and terrible countenance which came upon him like a storm-cloud of judgment. The sister, knowing well who came, for she had heard of the man and seen him, had no fear for herself, but began with trembling cheerfulness to put up her long hair, and to make the best face she might of nothing being amiss.

The woodman, who would ever see more than folk thought he had wit to perceive, felt his anger warm against the brother in measure with the sister's endeavour to cloak his wickedness.

"We—we did but play," she stammered. And the woodman looked at her until she let their lids fall between her eyes and his.

"Come here," he said to the brother; and the boy obeyed with what courage he might.

"What would you do?" asked the girl, her voice sharp with fear.

"I will whip him," said the woodman.

" 'Tis not your business, sir," she answered boldly.

"You are the first," he answered, "to tell me that a nasty and needful task is not mine."

The sister then changed her footing.

"I am sorry, sir," she said, "that I spoke falsely. And I am sorry my brother is wayward and unkind. It is true he did hurt me a little. But it will be pain much worse, be very sure, sir, if you should beat him."

Between her eyes and his there was now no screen, and for a moment he was lost, as in a blue pool of great sweetness and wonder.

Drawing himself to the shore again:

"I will not hurt him," he said. "But he must come with me to my hut in the woods. To-night I will speak with him. I will also feed him well, and he shall sleep warm. To-morrow he shall come home."

"I will trust him to you, sir," said the girl; and watched the two men as they passed into the road and out of her sight.

Next day the brother returned with face and heart so changed that his two women marvelled.

Now the king of that country had sent messengers into all parts to tell in the market-places and from house to house his need of soldiers for a war that there was. And in that village it was held great honour to wear the king's coat and to fight in his fighting; yet the mothers and the other women were not always willing that their men should leave them for those great dangers of life and limb.

So this poor mother, when her son said his purpose was for the war, fell, between pride and sorrow, into a great trembling and tears. But go he must, said her son, because the great woodman had said it.

"What said he?" asked the sister.

"That it would make me a man," answered the boy.

"You have no duty to the woodman," said the mother.

"The woodman's words, and his good face," said her son, humble for the first time, "have changed my heart. He tells me the King's army will teach me obedience and give me knowledge of my own littleness in the world. I would begin by obeying the man who has been best to me."

So to the wars he went, leaving more happiness behind him than ever he had brought.

Then his sister kept her cows many days in the river meadow. And when at last the woodman's feet, walking against prudence, took him once more by the longer road between his cottage on the forest's border and the village, the girl stood by the ditch where the hedge was thin and called to him. And he answered by leaping so easily across to her that her eyes were wide in astonishment, and of a shining blueness very deep and soft with her gratitude.

When she had told him their joy of the change wrought upon her brother, she must show him how her beasts had cropped the grass of that small meadow very close, in the days while she had waited for his passing; and where lay the pasture to which she must lead them on the morrow.

Few days, therefore, went by without a meeting, and the girl came to love with all her heart the man that had loved her since ever he saw her fingers busy with the loosened hair, the while she lied to him, covering her brother's unkindness.

So one day, when she had said that he was all the world to her, and he, that she was to him all the sky with sun, moon and stars to the bargain, she took him to her mother; and that sad and sickly woman had great joy in this man for her daughter, and said she might now die in peace and even happiness, should her boy but first come back to her from the wars.

But, after a long winter which had hindered work upon the new house the woodman must finish before taking to him his wife—a winter which drew away much of the life that was left in the old woman—there came news of a battle of the King's forces with his enemy's; and hard upon this a royal letter to the headman, setting out the list of those from that village who had died in the great victory. And our woodman, when he had read that list, believed he had sent a boy to his death.

But the soldier's sister said to him:

" 'Twas a man you sent, beloved; the wastrel would by this, but for you, have been an evil thing, to leave an evil name when he should die, whether in bed or ditch!"

But the mother, though she was still gentle and good to the woodman, and had in all her life never blamed a man for the good he had done, yet wept for not seeing her son again, and set her heart upon dying so soon as she might.

Now the woodman believed that the sick woman would have better health and more pleasure of life, if he could, in wedding the daughter, take the mother to dwell with her in the new house on the higher ground by the verge of the forest. So he and his men worked double tides, and had soon all things in readiness for marriage and flitting.

But the woman died in her sleep the night after he had told her what should be done on the morrow.

Back from the place of burying he took the daughter to her empty dwelling, and his heart was sore for her. Awhile they went in silence; but for all the maid's sorrow, his stolen, sideway glancings found great tranquillity in her countenance.

So, speaking at last,

"There is peace in your face," he said.

"And in my heart," she answered.

"Are you not afeard to be alone?" he asked.

"I am not alone, while you think of me," she said. "And when we shall be close, never again to part, why, I shall have my mother and my brother too. For you of all the world did them most kindness. And you will talk to me often of them, will you not?"

That he surely would, he said, so often as he or she should have them in mind.

Then a cloud came over his face, and she would know what troubled him.

"I but wonder," he answered, "that you do not fear me."

"Fear you? Oh, no," said the girl.

"And what of the village folk, child? If it be not fear of me that they feel," he said, "I know not how I should call it."

Now the girl did not frown upon others' fearing what she worshipped and could yet in a measure rule. So she answered him:

"It is your courage, your size, your strength—if fear they have. It is thinking on what you might do to one that should wrong you."

"Ay," he said. "Some of them know. They remember not one or two things only that I did, when I was younger than you to-day. There is in me"—and he touched his breast— "something evil, child, which would in those days break into flames—black flames with bright edges—and thereafter I scarce knew what I did, until it was done."

30

Afire with curiosity, she stopped in her walk and looked up in his face.

"Do they come now? I mean, those black flames?" she asked. And her lover not answering, "I have not seen them," she said.

"And shall not," he swore stoutly. "The last time, if it did not wholly kill them, yet taught me the trick to hold myself quiet till they should creep back into their den."

"Where is that?" asked the girl.

"In the bad side of my heart, I think," said the man sadly.

She laid a hand on his breast.

"Great names you have, dear man," she said, "for a fit of cross temper! What kind of wrong is it will bring this upon you?"

His eyes, while he answered, were cast down, so that she could not be sure whether it were shame or a brooding concern for the proclivity of his nature which hid them from hers.

"Some men hold themselves the safer," he said, "by making all the smaller things of life their intimate property—baggage, as it were, for the whole journey. To me a few things only are very much mine. A man might have my coat, or my house (till I built for you, child!); but he may not touch with the axe a tree I have marked to stand, nor pluck my flowers, nor use this knife in my belt that my father used, nor look angrily on my dog—"

And there he stopped, as one checked by evil recollections.

Softly she asked him:

"It was, then, the dog—that last time?"

And the woodman nodded.

"Tell me," said the girl.

"I was a boy—seventeen years. He was a man, and should have been the stronger. We stood on the wharf behind the market hall, watching the flood-water racing down. He kicked my dog, and I flung the man far out into the stream. Although my strength is now doubled, I could not to-day fling his weight half the distance, unless—"

"The black flames?" whispered the girl, worshipping the man and his power, black flames or none.

And again he nodded.

"But he did not drown?" said she.

"How can you know?" he asked in surprise.

"You leapt in and pulled him ashore, swimming greatly in that dreadful torrent. I know, woodman," she said, "because I know you."

"It is true enough. Yet do you not know me," he answered.

"He was cruel to the dog," she replied, making excuse for wickedness in him she loved.

"And even so you prove my word," he retorted. "It was not 'a dog.' Should I kill a man for the wanton hurting of a speechless animal—well! But 'twas *my* dog, and the wrong and the insult were to *me*. That is the black flames.

"So was I well-nigh a murderer—am such, perhaps. And there is another thing."

The girl's hand was on his arm, and when he paused, she shook the arm, to get from him the end of the story.

"Had he been a swimmer—such a poor swimmer, even, as are most here about," said the penitent, "I should, I verily believe, have stood watching him struggle till the river took him out of sight. It was the helpless, splashing foolishness of the man which cleared away those black things. And then—oh! the fight it was to bring him ashore! And there in the water I thought; if he had kicked my dog as we stood upon the hill road, and I had flung the man into the ravine! Could I then have fetched him back by any strength of body or goodwill of mind? So, as I swam, I vowed that never again—"

She saw him wipe the sweat from his face, and had great pity on him, so that she put an ending upon his unfinished words.

"That never again shall the black, spiked flames flicker their fiery edges? Truly," she said, "they shall not, for I will do you no wrong, and will stand so close that none other shall."

"If you do me no wrong? Say, rather, if none harm you!" cried the woodman: for he was beside himself with love.

"Yet were you gentle with my brother in his naughtiness toward me."

"Then," said the woodman, "you were not mine."

And the girl fell silent, till her lover left her in her quiet house.

Seven days, said their custom, must pass between burial and wedding, and upon the day next before the marriage-day the groom should not speak with the bride. But the woodman, in the dusk of the evening of that seventh day, was drawn by hunger of love to her neighbourhood, and for an hour watched her door and lower window, where a candle shone, in hope to see her face before he slept.

Now and again there was movement of coming and going in the house, voices and shifting of the light.

In speculation idly born of weariness, he asked himself what friend had she chosen to lighten her last lonely hours. But the voices rising a little, he could hear well hers that he loved, and a lower, fuller note, that came, he was sure, from no woman that he had heard before.

"She will fetch her candle with her, when she comes to the door to bar it for the night," he said to himself, "and I shall see her face lit from below, as when I left her so often."

So he moved from his hiding into the pathway to her door, trusting in the darkness.

This brought him into better earshot, and he heard more clearly the voice that was now surely no voice of woman. And the small black flames, edged with a glow as yet but of a dulled purple, covered the whole floor of his mind.

He had not yet reached her door, when he heard once more the man's voice, telling, in words of love, his joy to be come in time.

The flames flickered higher, bright of edge.

To the woodman the words "in time" could have but one meaning: it was as if he had heard from the girl's very mouth that there was a man with her that was more than he.

Despite the smell of death in his heart and the black flames in his mind, he had kept, until the house was entered, a measure of self-governance. But in the light of the one candle he saw the woman so nearly his wife wrapt in the arms of a man.

The man's back was towards him—a figure tall, slender and well clothed. Worse even than the arms clasping the girl's body was the terror in her blue eyes regarding him over the strange shoulder. Half her face he saw, and all that was not eyes was white like white stone.

The lover could not know that the awfulness of his own countenance had stricken the woman with fear so great that speak in time she could not.

As if through a loop-hole framed by the bright, dancing edges of his forked and quivering blackness, he saw her face and the man's back.

In a moment he had him by the left shoulder and swung him round so that they came face to face. But the woman, swayed aside, still clung to the right arm which had been round her body.

The woodman found his knife in his hand—the knife he had told her was once his father's. To kill the man he lifted it high, avoiding the clutch of fingers.

But in the same moment the girl, with great strength of fear, came between; and the knife, driven with force which might have severed links of steel mail, went slanting downward through the soft breast and yet more tender heart.

When again he could see, what he had done lay without life at his feet.

After awhile he looked up, in dull search of what he had purposed killing, and the eyes which met his were those of her brother whom they had thought dead in battle.

Then the woodman offered the bloody knife, which had been his father's, to the man that might have been his brother, asking for death. But the soldier would not.

"I give a worse doom," he said. "You shall live until life shall kill you."

The judge of that village heard the tale, very plainly set forth by the dead maid's brother.

"That is your story," he said, and turned to the woodman. "What have you to say to it?" he asked.

"It is mine also," said the woodman.

"It is but just to bear witness," said the soldier, "that the blow was not meant for my sister."

Having pondered awhile,

"Killing, nevertheless, was his intent," said the doomsman. "And even in such case as he vainly imagined, a man may not slay until he knoweth."

The doomsman again weighing the matter in a silence yet longer, the soldier spoke once more.

"After I leave it in this hour," he said, "I shall not set foot in this place again. So I will beg you remember that this man, though he has wounded the joyous present and slain the innocent future, has hurt most of all himself."

And so left them and that village, riding out to the world where he might forget the sister that he loved and the man that had made him the second time.

But the woodman spoke while the judge in careful doubt yet pulled at his beard.

"My doom is set already, sir," he said, "by her brother who now leaves us. I would have had him slay me, but he said that life, not he, must do that."

"So be it," said the judge. And so it was.

In the house he had built for her; the house he would never let the maiden see until it should be hers: "For it is not fit to be called a house till you shall be its mistress," he had told her; in that house, with the heath in front, and the soft, strong woods behind it, the house all filled with the dead pictures painted in the night-time between tired eyelid and sleepless eye; in that house the rest of his life was spent.

His work as Tree-master for that village was done as well as of old. None in subjection to him had ever a word against him, but that he had never two words where one would carry his meaning.

The village folk, as a new generation arose, called him by a name which signifies: "He that hath slain." They said that he lived without speech; and when he walked down the street or crossed the market place, a hush like a billow of silence would roll before and after him, tongues tied and eyes following the sacred wretch whose passion on a day long past had lost him all the good by which men live.

If two women, even, were at strife, they would fall silent on the word: "The slayer comes!" and often, it was said, would forget or forego their broil.

His sorrow, though it would seem thus upon occasion to salve almost sacrificially their daily and common woes, yet made the gaunt man in no wise dear to that people. There was a gulf between. None would have spent an hour with him but of necessity. Few cared to walk by his house in the hours between sunset and sunrise, and none shared with him its ghostly emptiness, until, in his fiftieth year, the burning sickness fell upon him.

There came then a night when the fire in his bones, as he called his malady, burned so sharply that no sleep, he thought, would ever come to him until there should be no more of him to burn. And for this he was the sadder in fearing to miss, for even one night, a certain haggard dream which seldom failed him.

For he would ever, sometime in the sleep of his night, dream thus, and never knew within his dream that he had so dreamed before:

That he lay waking in his bed; that from beyond and beneath his window came a little groaning sigh, with no gruffness in it; that he arose, lit his lantern and went out to see what woman or child might he in trouble. That out there upon the grass he found her whom he had stabbed with his father's long knife; that she lay as she had lain in her mother's house, the thick-twisted hair broken loose sidewise upon the ground, the gown torn away on the left side, as it had hung when the brother gave over staunching the wound; but in his dream the blood still welled up and flowed warm over the delicate whiteness of the bosom.

But when in his dreams he had borne her indoors and laid her on his bed, it was no woman, living or dead, that he saw and touched, but an image of stone, cold and white; and from the cleft high up on the breast not blood, but clear water trickled.

And then he would wake; and the life in him went on with its work of death.

So for twenty and more years had he dreamed, eleven nights at least of every fourteen. And each day he hoped that the night would bring this refreshment of his passionate memory to tear his heart yet again. While it tore him, never was it an old dream, but always a new thing alive.

Now this night, when for the fire in his body he might not sleep, he heard the cry of one whimpering and moaning beneath his window. Could it be, he thought, that he but dreamed the burning pain and his own wakefulness, and that here was the beginning of his dream, come in due course?

Nay, for never in this dream had he dreamed of dreaming, but always of things that were.

Dreaming or waking, cold chasing heat down his backbone, while ever his head burned hotter, up he got himself, made shift to light his lantern and went out—to find no dear horror of maiden blood and white, dying beauty, but the crumpled body of a woman, old, and wrinkled of face.

The night being cold, her clothes rags, and her strength almost naught, he could but bring her within.

He roused the fire and warmed the broth in the pot, and, when she was in a measure comforted, the old woman looked up at her host out of cunning little eyes which showed not yet any gratitude.

"You are sick, sir," she said, "and rather need my care than I yours."

Little trouble had she to get him to his bed, but not for many days could she fetch him out of it. And when at last he had something of his strength again, he asked her, would she stay with him.

"I am a bad old woman," she replied. "One town endured me while I was young, but now no small village but sends me to the next."

"You have been good to me," said the woodman. "And I also am an evil man."

"Are you not called the Slayer?" she asked. And the woodman nodded.

"Justly," he said.

"I have heard. You are not evil," declared the old woman; and stayed with him until he died.

Each time that she nursed him in his ever returning sickness did she feel greater love to him, so that by the time of the Elf's laughing on the village green the woodman was become as her own son to this old woman that had never borne child.

Often when the sickness took him had she feared it was the last sickness; but when the last sickness came, she knew it at once and surely. And the red-rimmed eyes grew sweeter by the tears she shed in secret.

One night he said to her: "Your gaze is like my mother's."

So for that one time she wept a little in his presence.

Of the man himself, she knew what he was; of his history, that in sudden rage of jealousy he had killed what he loved, and never had even tried to forgive himself. And also with his nightly dream had she an uncertain acquaintance, from words which would come at times out of his slumber, when the fire of the sickness was hot in his body.

Upon the night of laughing the breeze blew from the south. The woodman's house, which he had built for the wife that never stood inside its door, lay on the slope to the north of the village, between timber and meadowland, so that two or three, perhaps, of the joyous bubbles drifted towards the forest, to break over the house at its edge.

The old woman, watching her sick friend, heard a note, once, twice, even thrice, she used afterwards to maintain, of a music never known before; a music one may never forget; a music with a meaning new and all its own; but to tell the meaning words had not then been fashioned.

While she listened for more (but no more came to her) the woodman opened his eyes, and found a smile on the wrinkled lips bent over him. And on his the old woman saw its answer.

"What has happened?" he asked.

"I do not know," she answered. "There was a sound—wondrous sweet—as if the world should be made anew. What befell you in sleep, my son?"

For so would she call the woodman; but only in time of his sickness.

The great eyes in the drawn face shone to match the curling of the lips which smiled on her.

"In my dreaming," he began, "—but you will not understand, for you do not know the dream that I have had every night since I killed her—every night but a few blank ones, with a black day to follow."

"I know the dream—if it be the same you babble of in sleep, when the burning holds you."

"It is the same dream—always the same," said the sick man; "always until to-night."

The old woman, eager with love, leaped over her master, as she ever called him when he was up and about, and spoke whisperingly, patting her hand softly upon his blanket.

"When you had her into the bed to-night—to-night in your dream," she asked, "was the beautiful white breast turned to carved stone, and the red blood from its wound to thin water, very cold?"

"To-night in my dream," said the lover, "I seemed in the garden, barefoot in the snow. At first I could see her nowhere. But even while I slept I remembered for the first time in all the years of that dream, what it was I came for, and where it should be found. And, still in my dream, even where it should be, there it was; for amongst the snow, and by that hard for the eye to perceive, lay the carven image I had never yet seen outside my door. Now, at first I could not raise that marble counterpart of her."

For a little the woodman was silent. But the old woman waited; for she would as soon have cast a stone at a butterfly as risk by a word the true passage of that dream.

"I was a strong man, twenty years ago, mother," he said at last, in a voice he might have used to his own, "and should then have made little of lifting her measure in marble. In my dream to-night, each time that I essayed to raise her from the ground, a little of the old strength would come back to the older limbs, until at last I bore the stiff image in my arms and laid it where it was wont to be.

"Now, to do this," continued the dreamer, "the lantern must stand in the snow without. But as I laid her down here, there was no wetness of water on my fingers—the water, I mean, which was always the blood of that stone wound. I was amazed, and, thinking that you cannot shame marble with even a murderer's fingers, I passed my hand over that wounded left side of her from the shoulder downward. And there was not to be found any wound—no cleft in the marble smoothness at all."

After yet another waiting, the old woman heard more.

"I must needs see the truth of what my fingers had told me," he said, "and went (in my dream) for the lantern. And as I came back through the door, there was a sound that was a music and a wonder, sharp at first, like the breaking of bonds; then ringing long, and swelling, and afterwards curling away like coils of a woman's hair, blown by the wind-sweeter and ever more inward to the heart, mother, until it was gone."

"I know it," said the old woman, nodding. And her eyes were like young eyes.

"Once more I heard it," said the woodman. "And this time it minded me of the bubbles I used to blow from a hollow reed, when I had dipped the end in my mother's washing pool." And he laughed a little, never knowing that he had laughed never before.

"I'll be bound you heard it once again," said the old woman, eager with her own hearing.

"I do not know. For the second sounding brought me with my lantern into this chamber," he answered, "to find no cold image, but a woman sleeping, with no blood nor wound upon her. While I gathered the torn smock to cover what no longer showed my wicked mark, her eyelids were lifted, and she saw me and put out her arms to take my head in her hands."

This time the silence was long, so that the old woman, peering close at last, saw that the sick man slept again.

With a chuckling sound like the false dawn of laughter, she fell herself asleep, to awake, she knew not whether after hours or minutes, at the touch of the woodman's long meagre fingers upon her arm.

"I have seen her again," he said, and his eyes were like hot stars. "She spoke with me, and I have learned much. Next time that I sleep, I think I shall know all that there is."

Softly again he laughed, and the old woman asked why he did that.

"I do not know. It eases the strife that there is between the new things and the old, and makes them one, I believe. It came, you know, with the sound that was a bubble, ringing so purely. You did hear it yourself, mother, and must know that it belongs to the surprise and the uncouthness that there is when the enemies and the contrary things join hands, and joy sucks life at the breast of sorrow. To-night—even now, in a dream—I asked her, why did she keep me waiting so long, and she said: 'Because never before could I get through, dear woodman. But to-night,' said she 'a great thing for the world—for all the worlds—has happened, so that a man shall see two seeings at once, what his own eyes tell him, to wit, along with what his fellow sees with other eyes. And the two seeings will at first clash, giving each other the lie, and thereafter mix into an unity more true than either.'

"And then she tells me how this new thing has served her and me. For through all the years she had been trying, she said, to come at me; but never, for all her love, could draw near enough to tell me the words that should ease her pain, and mayhap mine: for that, so soon as, in my dream, she was within hail, she ever found that I could answer in no other way than to find her as she was when she lay dead by my hand; or as an image cut from stone, when I would hold her in my arms. But to-night, when she perceived those three bubbles of laughter—"

"Laughter? What is laughter?" asked the old woman.

" 'Tis a name she gave to this harmony of discords, mother. When she saw those three bubbles sailing our way, she made great haste to outstrip them, and reached us, old woman, in time for my dream and the laughing to meet."

"And what was it she told you at last, after twenty years?" asked his nurse, in the curiosity of love, but with the voice of age wheedling a child.

Gleeful astonishment and the desire to arouse the same mixture of emotions in the old woman set the woodman laughing again, so that she took the infection and laughed with him.

"All those years," he said, "has she been constant in purpose and endeavour to get across, if but to ask my pardon: saying that the crime was more hers than mine. She had well understood, she said, from the tale of the black flames, that she ran in danger by loving me, and loved me the better for the danger. And since she knew I purposed watchfulness, so had she, in her simple maid's way, sworn that no cause would she ever give to those little flames for leaping up and covering all things with a screen between my eyes and the truth. 'Dost remember,' she asked me to-night, 'the fierce grey wolf that haunted the coppice above our old house, and how you would watch the night through and every night, until you had killed him and brought me his pelt? And all lest I should endure an hour of fear in the loneliness of my brother's being at the war. And yet, when my brother came back as from the dead, I forgot you, beloved, and all the little black wolves with fiery tongues, of which you had told me so little a while before. Had I but sent you word the boy was come! So,' she said to me, 'I must have your pardon, beloved.'

39

"Upon this, having learned already a little of the new fashion, I fell a-laughing, that she should talk of wrong done to me. Whereafter we forgave each other, and in each other's arms were shaken with this new humour of the spirits, until she drew herself away to a distance proper for our eyes' meeting, and said:

" 'Truly, this laughter is the very fellow of love, so well do they work together.'

"Thereupon, to hear more of her voice,

" 'Work?' says I. 'And to what end?'

" 'Surely, now,' she answered, 'they do work together, like a team well matched, to make a man see both sides of a thing.'

"Then she halted a little, to better her saying thus:

" 'To make him, I mean, in a single vision, see all sides of everything.' "

Short of breath, with the pain hotter than ever in his bones, the woodman asked for drink. And the old woman gave him a cup of her wine and honey, in which were steeped subtle seeds: and while he drank in slow mouthfuls,

"Did not this sweet ghost," she asked, "tell more things which are good to be known?"

"Much more she told me," said the woodman, smiling for memory: dreams being, like houses, greater within than without. "But I have no time for the telling of them, mother."

"Time?" she answered. "Why, time is all before you."

But he shook his head, setting down the cup.

"The drink, like all you make for me, is good," he said. "There is no time, I say, because I must go back to her. For I said to her, could we but come at her brother, we might get him into this humour of laughing and loving, all three of us together.

" 'He leads the King's soldiers in a great battle to-night,' she answered. 'If we should be near that place early to-morrow, there might be a meeting contrived.'

" 'If you will guide me, I will come,' said I.

"So she sent me out to tell you of my gratitude—"

"Gratitude!" said the old woman, drooping her head.

"And of my love, with hers, lest I be long away. Now I will sleep," he said, "for that is my way to her."

So the woodman slept, breathing softly and free. And the old woman sat by his bed with no sleep, but a great quietness upon her.

Before the dawn he stirred a little, and laughter came out of him. And the old woman listened to the sweetness of it until the laughing and the man's spirit in the same moment left her.

At noon she told the headman of that village how the ghost of his dead lover should take the woodman where her brother was fighting the King's enemies. And three days later they had news that the King's Chief Captain, that was the slain woman's brother, had died in victory two hours after the sunrise which followed the Elf's laughing upon the green.

# V

## Innocence

There was in that village a man of good estate that had, for all his family, a daughter, loving and beautiful.

Now, when her full growth was come, he found that his declining years had crept upon him with the same stealth; and, desiring her love and service for himself alone, he would, if any youth should come asking the maiden in marriage, send him away uncomforted.

So it came that, when she was a maid no longer, her fault was discovered to her father, and he said to her:

"Daughter, where is thy virtue?"

But she found no answer for him, and he drove her from his house, saying to her:

"Return again when thou canst bring thine innocence with thee."

So she went from him, hiding her face.

But, after days very many, there came a knocking at night upon the door which had shut out her tears.

And the father rose and went to the door and opened it, so that the light of his candle fell upon the face of his daughter.

"I have come to you again," she said. "And I have brought what you bade me bring."

Then, while she unwound the outer robe from her shoulders, the father, having forgotten the words of his bitter saying, asked of his daughter, what was that?

"I have brought my innocence," she answered, and showed him the head of her little child, cushioned on her breast.

Thereupon, as if in response to some tender jest in her words, there arose behind her from the village green the Elf's strange and beautiful laughter.

So long as it lasted they stood as men wrapped in a vision. But the babe opened his eyes, and flung out soft fists, knit like a man's. And when the Elf's laughter was at an end, the little child took up the tune to such sweet purpose that his grandsire must needs join in the catch.

And the laughing was wholesome in him, driving much bitterness and evil from his heart; so that he put his arms about daughter and grandson in a single embrace and drew them into his house.

"Innocence indeed!" he cried. "I believe he hath enough for the three of us!"

# VI

## The Rainbow Gamut

In that day and that village there was a boy that had music in his heart, running out by lips and fingers.

The mouth which his mother gave him, and the pipe which an old shepherd had taught him to make and to play upon, he used for repeating and varying the simple melodies of that countryside. But when he had been listening to the few singers and many birds and waters of those parts for some nine years, he began the making of what he called "tunes of his own."

If the dim form of a melody should come to him of a morning between sleep and waking, his lips would at once be pursed for the sweet, broken whistling which would trickle from them while he pulled on his clothes, caught up his reed pipe and padded barefoot down the stair and out into the street.

Custom had taught his father and his mother to endure this truancy with compassion, rather than to correct their little son with stripes. The mother feared him somewhat lacking in his wits, while the father, though vexed at heart that the child was not as other children, was yet now and again touched with an inkling that his son varied from the general rather by more in his head than by less.

Escaped, the child would run to a place which he had and kept secret from all but the old shepherd that had taught him the pipe. This place was a narrow glade in a wooded hollow, through which there flowed a little stream, widening to its meeting with the river.

Sanctuary gained, he would, maybe, roll himself like a joyous dog three times on the close, emerald-green turf; then rise and trot down, by a cleft in the bank, to the brook's margin of fine sand, and there sit squattingly to listen awhile to the delicate noise of the stream.

Anon he would fetch from his pocket, one after another, seven small things that he had, which were the tools of his infant art.

To his fancy, every tone of the gamut he used had its peculiar colour; and as his hand would encounter first in his pocket a lump of brick, once jagged, but now by use rounded smooth at the edges, he would sing a pure, low note, which gained volume and surety as his eyes met the redness of that morsel of burnt clay in his palm. A small, three-cornered slab of green marble would come next; a blue shard from a broken pot, a gold button that he had found and treasured for its plangent yellowness, a bit of glass with a tincture of purple in its transparency, and, at the tail, two pebbles, sad-coloured enough but for certain specks which he alone could find in their greyness: for, as he drew forth these two last, he would lick each delicately with darting tongue, to disclose the freckles, of deeper yellow upon the one, of deepest blue upon the other, which had given them privilege of proxy for the lacking tints in his rainbow gamut.

Laid on the white sand in a heap, he would regard the seven for a while, thinking rather than breathing his new melody. And next would begin, with softly whistling lips, a game, it seemed, of ordering and re-ordering his coloured tones.

And when, after more shifting of his pieces on the sand, and renewed conning over in notes surpassing any bird's for sweetness, the boy was content with this first chapter of his seven characters, he would fetch water, wet a strip of sand therewith and, in the order now determined, would press each character down upon the wetness and remove it again, leaving the imprint of a shape which he could never see without its colours coming also into the music-wise mind of him. The first chapter, then, thus imprinted, there he was with his tools all free to pursue his recording.

And at last, his emblems cyphered out in long lines across the shore of that little cove, leaving whistling and singing, he would stand erect and fetch out his pipe; thereafter to strut to and fro, body upright but eyes downcast to read, playing his "new tune" with full volume of breath and tube, until he knew it by rote of heart, and might go home to dinner with a new possession, the red note jostling solemnly, martially or sadly with the strong blue, the lambent yellow, the patient green and all the others whose symbols danced, he would fancy, in his pocket.

His mother would watch her one child's eyes as he ate, and say afterwards to his father:

"His strange passion, husband, doth at least make our son happy."

"When his melody is stirring and noble—ay!" the father would answer. "But when it is plaintive, ghostlike, and even lovesick, he pulls a long face enough."

" 'Tis not so sure the sadness is even then properly his," the woman once replied. "For he makes but what he can unmake, and has his joy of the beauty there is in it—and of the making too."

"Then is he not the witless thing you have at whiles held him. But sometimes," said the man, "when he thinks himself unmarked, I do see him sad indeed. He has then the face in small of the man that cannot find, nor put its name to the thing he most needs."

"When he finds it—" began the woman.

"Then, mayhap," said the father, "I shall find him."

46

Though he had little care for music, he had great love of his son; and this led him to believe what he could neither hear nor touch.

Now, had the boy heard these sayings, he would, in his twelfth year, have known them for true.

The music he had heard from others was little, and of but three moods: warlike music, of strife and of conquest, which should rouse even your coward to the courage of a moment; the music of longing and desire; and the music of death, loss and sorrow.

But his growing heart desired something more—something which should flout, mix with, disdain, and yet upon occasion reconcile all the rest.

Each of these musics that he knew was, he perceived, without words to say it, *my* strife, *my* victory, *my* longing, *my* love, *my* loss, *my* sorrow; and he loved them all, and all that he himself had made in their pattern.

But!—and his hand would feel the precious medley in his pocket, and he would wonder of what colour, if he should find it, would be an eighth note in his gamut.

Sometimes the children would make him pipe for them. With the first kind of piping they would fall into step, fiercely joyous, and threatening great things with little swords and javelins made of wood. The second kind would send the girls apart in couples or alone; but the boys would leave him playing to the air.

As for the music of dole—the boys would say it was no music at all, but a wailing of cats at night-time; while the maids would weep and ask for more of it.

So he would go to his sanctuary and well-nigh break his small heart, now and again, with reaching after melody that should be for all men at once and in one.

There came a night which was the first in his life wherein he could not sleep. And he saw through his window that the world was a-shine with the moon, and he had a great longing for his stream and his grass and the white sand of his cove, to see them in that light. So he crept from his room under the thatch, and softly down the stair to the street, never waking a sleeper in that house.

A little way he ran, and was upon the village green, making to cross it. So it fell out that he alone of that village was close upon the Elf when the great laughing came, and heard even to the last vanishing thrill of the last echo all that to be heard there was.

What he may have seen—if see he did—was never known: for if man or woman would ask him of that, he would smile and fetch out his pipe; and while that was at work was no time for questions, except the forgetting them.

47

I think, if we had him here, such as he was then; and if we asked him, not of the Elf's person, but of his laughter, its nature and its qualities, he would answer us more directly—but still with his pipe, which might match, or even (so tradition has it) better a fit of laughter; but that he could not clearly tell us more than we know of little pointed ears, puckered face and bright, yellow-brown eyes.

But it is certain that the thing which he had lacked—of which his need had been so patent even to his father, a plain man to whom music was naught—it is certain that this thing came to the whistling boy that night upon the village green.

When the laughing was done, he was not even sad, but went back to his bed and slept.

Mother, father and son broke fast together, and while they ate, twice did the man ask the boy why he had no word to speak that morning; and twice the boy's whole answer was a smile.

Now, neither mother nor father had broken sleep for the Elf. So they marvelled what new manner of twisting the lips should this be on the child's face; but, finding in it kindness and no offence, made no matter of it.

Once again the father asked the question. And then,

" 'Tis because I think so hard, sir," says the son, "of how best to tell you a thing that I have heard. I must fashion my speech to a point in the garden." And so went out, to return very soon with his pipe at full blast. And the music he made for his father was of conceit so curious, of tricks so sweetly and shrilly surprising, that the father and the mother had first a great happiness in them; whereafter came tears to the mother's eyes, but into the father's breast and throat a great passion of laughing which hurt him, as not yet knowing its proper way out. Seeing, then, his father amazed and clutching at his throat, the son took his pipe from his mouth and flung back his bright head in a peal of laughter which was heard down the street and over the green, so that the shopkeeper and his workman, with others who had not slept through the night, thought it was the Elf come again.

With this leading, the father laughed full and easily till the tears and sweat ran down his face with the joy and movement of it; and when he had his breath in him again, he looked round him and found the world showing its old face, but with a new meaning shining through the features of it: so that, but for a weariness about his belt, he could have laughed anew at his old table for the mere four-leggedness of its aspect.

So he asked:

"What then is this new thing, my son, that you bring out of your pipe?"

The boy shook his head.

48

"I know no more, sir, than you," he said. "There was a sound last night which went to my heart, and some of it comes out again through my pipe."

"Is it then that thy music is changed, rather than thy father?" asked the man.

But the mother, whose face by now had a smile like the sun when the clouds are split, took up the answering:

"I think, my dears," she said, "that the change is in you both."

With the hearing of music and the practice of laughter, this man and this woman found their love to their son not merely to grow, but to blossom in new manners, day by day, of disclosing itself; so that seldom has a household of three held joy deeper or more radiant

The piper, in courtesy extreme, took father and mother in one day to his sanctuary: on that day, to wit, in which he completed, with his stones, shards and gold button, the cyphering of the melody which the Laughing Elf had set him a-whistling. It was to be, he told his father, a tune which must set all boys and girls of the village, until now so various in taste of his music, dancing, marching and singing as one.

" 'Tis very old, sir—all the bits," he said, tossing up blue emblem after green, with the gold button to follow twinkling in the sun, and watching them fall with soft thuds into the unwetted sand, as if he gambled to make a tune by chance:

"There's the war feeling, the joyous victory feeling, the pain feeling, the longing-ever-so-much feeling, the mooney-soft-happy feeling and the sorry sadness; but mixed, you will perceive, sir—joined, melted, linked into one tune for us all."

The father heard it, in the glade by the stream, piped in its perfection, full, tender, merry and assured. And he said:

"It is, indeed, built of the old bricks—but a new house, my son."

Now it chanced that this great music was first piped upon the village green on the afternoon of the day which brought to the village the news of the King's great victory over his enemies—that same great battle where died the high Captain whose sister had long ago been slain by her lover. And the music did so seize upon the hearts of that place that the elders stood round the green in ecstasy to hear its thrilling sweetness, and to see how all their children obeyed the law of this piping song, falling into ordered action of dancing, marching, whirling and singing, with other joyousness never before heard nor seen; and how never a one had any thought for himself nor his limbs until the piper would pipe no more.

The headman praised the piper to his father.

"Some spirit," he said, "hath taught him the notes to celebrate our victory."

And the little piper smiled, knowing that the victory was not the King's, but the Laughing Elf's.

# VII

## The Giant

In the nature of man is the lust of fighting; and into fighting one quarrelsome fellow may lead the crowd.

Villages, also by their nature, are famous for quarrelling; and since laughter is the worst enemy of hatred, it is little wonder that the worst quarrel which ever was in the village of our story should have burst from smouldering into flame before ever the Elf's new voice was uplifted.

Upon the slope of the hills which come down to its northern side lay a vineyard, and between the vines and the village were spread meadows and rich plough-land, which yielded to the winegrower much wheat and fed many beasts to add to the wealth of the wine stored in the cellars of the strong old house which looked out over its hedges upon the village green. And the master of these lands was a very good fellow indeed, and his wife kept the best inn there was in the village.

For neighbour he had on his right, as the houses faced, a man that was a smith as well as farmer, with good lands also, and a good man of his hands.

Now these two neighbours had grown, through various fortune, into friendship more intimate than was by either understood until the trial of it came.

The lands of this winegrower and this smith, touching where they touched the village, were yet increasingly divided and spread apart as they stretched back over the grassland and corn-fields between the village and the hills; so that they embraced and almost enfolded the smaller but well ordered and fruitful lands of a widow woman and her sons—a family honoured for its good neighbourship, and always tenderly entreated by the farmers of those parts for its past misfortunes; wherefore they did all agree together, some years before the Elf's coming, when there had been no little strife over boundaries and such matters, that this widow's landmarks should never more be called in question, nor her fields invaded by the cattle and dogs of any other grazier, nor by the huntsmen from the hills.

For among the little known, half wild men to the northward the nearest was a strange fellow whom many of that village feared. Yet, because by purchase, by trickery and by seizure this man's father and his father before him had increased their wide lands until their southward terms marched with the northward line of the winegrower's holding, the fellow claimed loudly to be of their race, and none said him nay.

So great was he of stature and bulk that some held him descendent from the old stock of savage giants. But the greater number said this could not be: for that the giants of their tradition were all stupid, and for the most part bad.

Now, this man, they said, was full of a strange kind of sagacity and dexterity for turning all thoughts and things of others to his own use and enrichment; and they said it was unjust indeed to call a man of such parts bad for the mere size of him, and for a trifle of surliness and grossness in his habits.

From this opinion, it is plain that many had forgotten how this big fellow's father had seized two goodly fields from the winegrower's father, and, because of the weakness of the King's government in that day, had kept those fields ever since for his own. But the winegrower and the winegrower's family remembered that robbery; while the blacksmith, for a certain soreness he felt that his own father had not gone out with his dogs and his servants to help his neighbour, had also that memory always in the private part of his mind.

Some few days before the Elf's laughing, this giant began in the village a very fierce and boastful kind of talking with all the farmers he would meet, of his right to this, and his power of that, and of his purpose to belabour all men that should stand in his path; until at last they began fearing some fresh quarrel, all of his making, soon to break out in blows. And the smith, meeting with the giant one day, told him in speech very plain, that he should not, in his captious passion of greed, pass by the easy way of the widow's fields to those of his neighbour the winegrower, nor to any other's.

"That," he said, in the end of some talking, "is what all have agreed."

And he stood swinging his sledge-hammer, looking the giant in the eyes so that he remembered how the smith's father had said the same in the old days; and how his own father had been afraid to come that way, and had brought his fierce dogs and savage men over the hills instead, when he came to make seizure of those two fields that were the winegrower's.

So he went away and fed his dogs and talked with his men. His dogs, which he called sheep-dogs to protect his flocks from thieves (but there was no sheep-thief in that region, save only on his own land), were animals with whom it seemed no sheep might find safety; and the tale ran that in winter, upon the hills bordering the distant confines of his domain, the giant was used to train them in man-hunting, using as quarry such of his servants as had chanced from time to time to displease their master.

With the manners and countenances of wolves, they were trained, like packs of hounds, to obedience resembling the ordered discipline of soldiers.

At dawn of the day next after he had spoken with the giant, the smith was roused out of his sleep by a great clamour which came from the low-lying fields of the widow's farm.

In less time than ever before he found himself out of his bed, half clothed and running, as he had run in his youth, towards the tongue of land which would have touched his own boundary, but for the brook; and which hugged, with no ditch between, the fields of the winegrower on this side, and of the savage giant upon that. And as he ran the smith twirled in his hand a great sledge-hammer as if it had been a twig.

But the giant's hounds had already killed the widow's two watch-dogs, and behind them the smith saw the wicked fellow himself, beating the widow's sons and daughters, whose courage to drive him and his rout from their fields was greater than their strength. For they were now, as the smith stood on his bank of the stream, already scattered and overthrown; which seeing, the smith was filled with wrath, so that, leaping the water, he laid about him wonderfully with his hammer among those wolf-like dogs; and the winegrower coming to his side with a hunting spear, they made brave show for a while, killing many hounds and wounding heavily some of the wild men that commanded the packs.

Yet were they before long almost whelmed by numbers; for their sons and their neighbours, their servants and their further townsmen were at that hour scarce out of their beds. So it came that these two landowners and their two brave house dogs, a pair of lusty dairy wenches that had been early abroad, with an old shepherd who had been waking all night, were forced across the stream towards the winegrower's strong old house, fighting hard between each backward step and the next, and killing many of the hounds that pressed hardest on their retreat.

But when the giant's fellows began crying aloud how they would soon burst into that house, drink the wine and carry off women, cattle and goods before burning it about the winegrower's ears, the noise of it got abroad, and men came out from every house with sticks and pikes, scythes and flails, and driving the wild men and dogs backward, saved the house for that time.

Yet was the fighting by no means at an end. For over the hills to the northward down the slope of the vineyard came a new parcel of sturdy rogues that were in some sort our giant's cousins and their aid bespoke beforehand.

So across the fields the fight grew hotter as the sun rose higher, and the smith sent his daughter on the best nag that he had to fetch a few cousins of his from the far side of the great river. So ever during the day of that fighting more men from afar came into it.

But near sundown, when the good men and their many friends were pressing mighty close on the giant himself, our smith came up with him, and caught him a great blow of his hammer on the side of the head; so that he fell his length and lay still.

By the time they had bound him hand and foot, the giant's men and such of his dogs as lived were chased out of sight over the hills.

"Let us hang him now," said the winegrower.

"Better keep him the night," answered the smith; "and if to-morrow his wits are in him, we will lay him in a waggon and take him to the King's city for judgment."

So they carried him within doors, and let him lie with a guard over him, while they gave wine and food to their departing friends.

But when these were gone and all was quiet under the risen moon, the giant's senses returned to him, and they gave him wine and food.

With eating and drinking, strength began so to swell again in the mighty body of him that his captors said, they two would watch beside him until sunrise, lest he escape and more mischief come of it.

The moonlit night, after the strife of that day, seemed peace indeed; and the two neighbours, friends closer than ever, sat, now talking, now silent, following, as friends should, each his spirit of thinking; until there broke over that silence the Elf's first laughter, for a wine, a balm and a colour to the spirits of all men.

The tide of this new thing, pouring itself into the hearts of winegrower and smith, kept them silent awhile with its sacred astonishment. And then from both hearts and out of both mouths the flood broke back again; so that when a pause came in their mirth, each found the other's right hand close in his own.

Then they saw their captive to be heaving and straining mightily against his bonds, and watched him curiously, until a fresh string of jewels from the Elf's throat set them laughing anew.

But this second outburst, it seemed, drove the giant into a great passion, whether of pain, or of anger; so that, after knotting himself all hunched together, he leapt to his feet with a vast and sudden bound, breaking in the same moment the cords which shackled wrists and ankles.

The smith reached for his hammer; but the winegrower stayed his purpose.

"Wait," he said, "until this bubbling melody shall come again. If he answer it as you and I have answered, old friend, we shall know there is in his gross carcase a man's heart. If not—"

For conclusion to his words the winegrower picked up the spear which he had used in the battle of the meadows.

As if the Elf had heard him, the laughter came again; beginning in soft, crooning rumblings, gentle as doves' talk of marriage on a spring morning, and passing through a riot of joyous surprises to the ringing of a scale of bells strung upon a cord swayed by the wind; note mounting above note without jar of shrillness, until silence came, not, it seemed, from lack of bells to carry on that sweet ascension, but from failure of mortal ears to answer the celestial pitch.

Hands upon weapons, eyes upon the giant's face, the two men waited. Twice before the Elf's laughter left them, the breast of the monster heaved with the great draughts of air that he fetched—breath which they hoped should issue again in some half savage yet consonant answer to the strange music.

Twice was the giant body convulsed, and twice the face distorted in agony of disgust. But when the last note died upon the ear which found in it no sweetness, the giant flung his arms wide and pitched forward, falling as a tree falleth, without bending.

To them, leaning over the huge carcase in search of the life which had left it, comes the winegrower's wife, asking was it an earthquake which had so shaken the house. And her eyes were full of the Elf's laughter, which had come to her in sleep; and her lips had new curves in them that made the winegrower kiss his wife before he answered her.

" 'Tis our prisoner that has been troubled in his dying," he said.

"Was it the strange sound—the music out there?" she asked; and laughed soft and murmuringly for the memory of it.

"Ay, madam," says the smith. "That sacred clamour got into him; yet could not issue again, but curdled upon his heart, so that he died!"

# VIII

## Fingers and Toes

There lived in that village a man and his wife that had a single child. Four years had she been there between them, a bond in truth, but sometimes in seeming a division.

For the child, being in some matters unlike to other children that they knew, gave to father and mother contrary qualms of anxiety. If this month she were plainly more tidy, more docile and more loving than any other little maid of her age in the village, the woman would say with tender arrogance that her lovekin would be a woman before her time and do all work about the house while mother should rest old bones in the chimney-corner. But the man, perhaps, would answer that the girl must needs, before she could claim even a child's fit knowledge, master a few more words of the speech she was so slow to learn.

Or, again, when she would for a month run afield for flowers and after butterflies, the mother would cry out that her little helper was changed for a wild, gadabout savage, getting naught but tangled hair and torn clothes; but the father, that she gathered, with her browned skin and stronger legs, a whole bookful of new words, and much fair knowledge that did hang by them.

Now in all this, she is not, perhaps, to us who are neither her father nor her mother, very different from other children; yet she had, almost from her birth, a practice which seemed to set her apart from those of her day and country: a custom, that is, of playing a certain game or exercise with her toes.

Sitting, whether on bed or floor, as naked as they would leave her, she would, in solemn contemplation, finger those blunt members until one came to hide them in stockings and shoes. And this distraction, in days when she was new to her shoeing, would at times take her tender spirit at a bias, raising clamour and resistance; yet was at other times accepted with a resignation which seemed to say that the practice of philosophy was at worst merely postponed.

"What does she think upon?" asked the mother, "when she fingers her toes?"

The father watched many days, until the mother had asked that question a third time. And then,

"I do not know, wife," he replied. "But I would counsel you, if you must come with that foot-harness between her and her mystery, to do it when it is the fingers which play the game."

"They are for ever playing it," said the wife.

"Not so," answered the man. "Watch and you shall see that at times she does toe her fingers. At such a time, let be until the hand take up again the business of tickling, counting and matching the fingers of her feet."

As if his words had been naught, the woman said nothing. But the man marked that there came to him no more cries and strugglings at shoeing time.

In the maid's fifth year, when she had more words than they knew, for the few that she used, the man and the woman had almost forgotten the mystery-game of toe and finger; but in secret the child played it still.

To tell all that lay behind this ritual would need not merely more knowledge than came to the Laughing Elf upon that night when Joy and Sorrow found Love standing hid beneath their elbows, but also more and better words than have yet been used by all the pens which that meeting did set a-scribbling; for we may give words to him that has words; but very great indeed is he who can give form to that which is but a-shaping.

This child, before other of her kind, was feeling, maybe, for the spirit which binds, endears and enlightens a worldful of likenesses and differences.

Her toes, when her fingers first found them, were a mystery—as like unto her fingers, let us say, as her father was like to her mother, as her sun was like to her moon. Yet were her fingers as different from her toes as her cat from her dog; and she would, in supreme essay at discovery of truth, strive to make the toes do her handling; and the way they went awkwardly about it would give her a pain—and a longing for a passion that she had not, nor yet her world.

Things were all separate things in her small house; and her spirit, perhaps, told her from far away that she needed a closeness, a belonging, a fusion which should bring all things into one happiness. And so—why, even the game of "This little pig went to market" gave the five little fellows that were, yet could not be, fingers, no fellowship at all; five separate fates, and not a bond in that family! For this maiden philosopher loved her bondage, would it but tie her enough.

So, with large, solemn eyes opened wide to catch all the moonlight that fell through her window, she sat, that night of the Elf's laughing, on the floor of her bedchamber, playing her game once more and trying to play it after a new fashion. But her spirit was heavy, and the big toes were both proud that night, and thought no good of the others, so small beside them. And the three middling toes had their heads together, affecting secrecy, and the little outside fellow of each foot was asleep, and it wasn't worth while to waken pigmy people so silly as they.

It was, however, a cult, rather than a pastime; wherefore she would not yet leave it.

Seizing an ankle in each hand, she bent the two white little feet, which would have been pink in the sunlight, towards each other until they were sole to sole, and not far from touching each other flatly.

"They will better understand each other, maybe," she thought, "than they understand fingers."

But though she forced each row of little pigs to bow until from the haughty toe to the sleepy one they touched each his counterpart, there was no satisfaction in it; although, with an effort, she made each toe in each company spread aside from his neighbour, and, with help from above, got the toes of the right into the spaces of the left foot as fingers of clasping hands are matched, it made but poor hugging; so that she was thinking herself as fond and silly as her feet and was almost of a mind to crawl again between blankets, when the Elf laughed.

Now this laughing was to the child like the breaking of bonds about the spirit within her; like the rising of a sun upon her inner world, like a bringing of all the aloof things together out of a dull lesson-book into a jolly picture. She did not know, until she remembered it in the morning, that the laughing came to her through the window, so freshly did it seem to arise from her own inward parts; and even when the morning came and the sun awoke her with hot kisses, she could not have told even her father whether the wild game of fingers and toes, which had been that laughter's first work, had been played before her eyes by her own fleshly little members, or behind her closed lids by the spirits of them: and she had wholly forgotten how and when she got again to bed.

But the game itself she remembered all her life better than all the words she ever learned could tell it—and remembered how it held her making a new noise like that noise which had made a picture for always of all the world.

There was one movement in that game wherein the toes all pretended themselves fingers, until the fingers, following the pattern, must needs ape toes; whereafter each party falls back into its own character, yet so expanding its proper quiddities as to make game each member of himself and his kind.

Again, some would be sick, or wounded, and come to health once more—die and revive—mourn, and leap back of a sudden to joy; until of their pranks there seemed no end. But the child well knew their beginning, and in the daylight she must needs make trial of others, whether they also had heard laughter.

So soon, therefore, as she perceived, by the voices behind the door which joined her chamber with her mother's, that her father was at the last of his dressing, the little girl scrambled from her bed and, clad but with her shift, pushed the door wide and flung herself headlong and full length upon the floor of the greater room, crying out and sobbing like one in pain, most natural and lifelike.

The mother was the quicker to pick her up; but the father comes running behind to comfort.

The little hands were at the eyes, to hide for yet a moment the dryness and the shining of them, while the groanings and sobbings of the breath still shook the little body.

And then of a sudden the child spread her arms abroad, showing a countenance radiant with its first full smile of triumph, and eyes a-fire with glee; and out of her throat burst a sound at first for all the world like a soft and musical cock-crowing, but sliding away from that into one cascade after another of pure treble laughter, to be broken only for breath to begin again.

While for a moment the mother thought that here was some new terror of disease or possession, the father was at once brought in mind of a dream he had had that night while he slept. And when the mother saw that there was joy, not sorrow in it, she too remembered the laughing she had thought a dream.

"The little good-for-naught mocks me," she cried, shaking the child, yet gently; but was very soon fain to leave that, for the impulse of drollery which seized upon her own inward parts and shook her strongly until its way out was found in laughter.

To see the pair of them so tossed in the wave of the new passion got the man very soon into a like helplessness of merriment, so that it seemed long before the three could come by a pause in which to wipe eyes and draw breath.

The child was the first to find words. Feeling herself for this time chief in the family,

" 'Twas in the night, my mother, when the moon shined on the floor," she said, and laughed three little "ha-ha's" with a "he-he" at the tail of them.

And the father asking what was it befell in the night:

"I heard it," she said, and laughed again, but doubtingly, as fearing misbelief. "Ha! ha! ha!" she quavered: "like that it was, indeed."

The man looked at his wife, she at him. A shadow of awe passed upon each face, to melt in smiles.

"I also heard this new sound, maiden, in a dream," said the man.

"And I, beloved babe," said the mother; and caught the child into her arms. "Was it that," she asked, "which did set thee, little one, to mocking father and mother with false tears?"

And then all fell once more into laughing, as if it were the finest jest in the world that the child had made; as, indeed, for that time it surely was.

"No," cries the little girl at last. "The good noise which makes me to shake, went at once into my toes and my fingers. It was, truly, the first time that fingers and toes did ever understand one another; so that they played a game together which fetched out of me, mother, the noise which had set them about it."

Then the father asked his daughter of the game which feet had played with hands to the tune of moonlit laughter.

So, saying "Thus it was," and "This way, then, my fingers and that my toes," the child rehearsed for them as best she might the game which she believed had changed the world.

Because the father at last, but the mother from the beginning, must laugh at these antics, the child laughed also to hear them. But her wise and secret soul knew that none would ever see that game as she had seen it; for, having seen it, she needed never to play it again, but merely, behind shut eyes, to remember that which had taught her, once for always, the eternal mystery of make-believe.

# IX

## Laughter and Love

Midstream, over against our village, the river embraced an island where lived, in a cabin of tree-logs, two brothers that were fishermen, huntsmen and fowlers.

All things in life they shared in such wise that each had his full property in everything. It was no mere half of island, house, nor boat that belonged to each; but each brother felt himself, in that he owned and was owned by the other, the more fully master of all three.

Never, then, since the mother of them died, had there been strife nor cloud of evil between them, and peace surrounded them as the river enwrapped their island.

Now, that stream came to them embanked by their own king's land upon both sides, after serving for many scores of miles above as boundary between his kingdom and the domain of a friendly prince. And this prince had for all offspring a daughter.

This daughter was as difficult for the prince to deal with as she was good for all the world to behold; so that at last, in a meadow between his castle and the river, he built, hard by the stream, a strong tower, with windows small and thickly barred, and its one door thirty feet from the earth. And when it was finished he bade his daughter come walking with him alone, and showed her the tower.

"It is an ugly thing indeed," says the Princess, when she had walked round it, "and the door is too high for my legs."

"In you may go, with care and a ladder, well enough," answered her father. "But out is another matter—when the ladder lies its length upon the grass."

The Princess, having a shrewd inkling of his intent, boldly tilted her chin, and told him, were she left in that tower and the ladder withdrawn, she would surely make her another and descend.

"I may give you occasion, my daughter," he answered, "of making good that boast."

"When, sir?" asked the Princess.

"Immediately upon your next disobedience," replied the Prince, and strode back to the castle.

The Princess followed pensively after him; for her head was full of imagining the great things that she would do.

Now one day, when, from seeing it often, she had almost forgotten that tower, the old Prince sent for his daughter and told her it was well time that she should marry. To this she made no answer, but stood to all seeming meekly before him; and indeed thus far she was in agreement with her father.

"Therefore," he went on, "have I chosen a husband for you," and named to her a certain nobleman of a region not far distant, yet of whom she had never had sight, nor so much as even heard tell. And when he had spoken, the father looked in his daughter's face and saw that it was stiffened with anger. For in her long thoughts she had told herself it was she who should choose. Yet she well knew that her father did but follow the custom of her house in choosing for his daughter. So, after a while,

"Tell me of him," she said, gently enough. "Is he handsome, and brave, and good?"

"Brave if he wed you, daughter," he said, scoffing. "Twenty years hence you may know what goodness is in him. For his person, you will make your opinion to-night."

"If he please me, sir," she answered loftily, " I will let him wed me to-morrow."

"To-morrow you will not wed," replied the Prince. "But in three days' time, if he do not reject you, the fellow shall espouse you, whether he please you or no."

Very wide the Princess opened her eyes, and the skin of her face was reddened from chin to hair. With no word of answer she turned and left him.

But her father knew that she heard the words which he sent after her.

"We sup with ceremony to-night," he said, "the young baron on my left, you upon my right hand. Be exact to the hour, and nobly arrayed."

But his daughter walked out into the deep woods, with rage in her heart that she was made a chattel between two men. For in her shape of thinking, men should be ranged orderly for a princess's choosing and picking.

Yet after a while anger languished in her, until she slept on a warm carpet of pine needles, under the straight, dark trees and dreamed of such a man as might choose and be chosen in the same stroke of time; and awoke at last to find herself prisoner to a party of her father's guard, sent out to find her in whatever covert.

Seeing that the moon was high, whereas she had fallen asleep under no light but the stars', she knew it was well past the hour of the fine supper she had been bidden attend; and of this she was glad, as a first advantage in the strife with her father. But when she found that the soldiers led her, not to the castle, but to the meadow by the river and the black tower with its door high above the ground, she neither wept nor feared, setting her mind at once on devising escape.

The tower reached, there was the ladder in place at the open door and at its head, reaching hand to her mistress as she mounted, a serving-maid of the castle, whom she knew and loved not.

There the soldiers left her, closing the door and drawing down the ladder to lie upon the grass.

Four rooms she found in her prison: that upon which the great door opened, with a kitchen beyond, a sleeping chamber for herself and another for her servant. In the first was a table pleasantly set with a white cloth; but her mind being solely upon escape from this tower, she turned at first disgustedly from the food. Reflecting, however, that an empty stomach is the worst companion of perilous enterprise, and that the table was of aspect kindlier than her sour-faced attendant, she fell to with a will which changed very soon to appetite.

When she could eat no more, she bade the woman clear the table of its furniture, and to make what meal she could in the kitchen. And when she was alone, the Princess peered out through the spying-shutter of the great door, and saw that an iron bolt on its outer side was pushed well home into its socket on the jamb, that the ladder was pulled down, and that a bare three yards of turf lay between the tower's base and the little stone wall against the near side of which the ladder's foot had rested when she came to her prison. But on the other side of that low wall the river, swelled with late rains, washed the stones well nigh to the level of the turf on this.

Midstream, as if it floated, with feathery willows for sails, lay a tiny island. And when she had done with thinking of the old fisher that slept there in his hut, and of his boats moored to the islet's further shore, she thought once more of the bolt upon the door, and of how she had never heard the noise of it sliding into the hasp, when the soldiers had left her prisoned. "It is well oiled," she said in her mind, "and should come out softly as it entered."

And so, her woman being still at eating and drinking in the kitchen, the Princess unwound from her waist the long silk girdle which was wrapped many times about her, and, grasping the ends in her left hand, she dropped the bend of the scarf very deftly from her right over the knobbed head of the bolt; and then, with her left hand reaching so far down as it might between the bars of the hatch, she drew hard upon the doubled band until the bolt left its hold upon the door-post.

No sooner had she recovered her scarf than her woman came back; when the Princess, refusing tendance at her undressing, sent her servant to bed; whereafter the haughty prisoner very soon retired to her own chamber, there to lie sleepless the better part of two hours; then rising, crept soft-footed to her servant's bedside, where she found the woman sleeping heavily. Thus the mistress contrived, without waking the sleeper, to steal her clothes and fetch them to her own room, where she bound them, all save the shift, into a bunch.

A second packet she then made of her own garments, whereafter she slept a little until it was dawn.

Rising before the sun, the Princess, clad in her servant's smock, went to the outer door, drew it open, and dropped her two bundles to the sward at the tower's foot.

But as she lifted her eyes from the grass to the water of the river, horror came over her of the leap which she purposed: a fear, not of the thirty feet downward, which she had rather wished forty, but of the ten feet outward which must be overpassed in her fall to reach the yielding safety of the stream.

Perceiving, however, that two women could not live, even in prison, with but a single shift between them, the Princess drew back as far as the room's width permitted, and ran swiftly to the doorway, leaping from its sill with a good heart and a bold outward curve in falling which brought her safely to the kind embrace of the water; whereafter, once risen to the surface and filled again with the sweet air of the morning, she swam, sure of courage, to the fisherman's hut.

Now, the young baron who had been summoned to espouse the daughter of his overlord had never yet set his eyes upon that Princess. He had hitherto felt little mind to marriage, and he had ridden to the castle pondering means and watching opportunity of avoidance. His knowledge of the father gave him little hope of the unknown daughter; but when he found that she had so little mind to him that she refused even supper in his company, he was at once taken with a notion to behold this rebellious Princess; and when he heard, from the Prince her father himself, that her disobedience had been punished with imprisonment in a lonely tower by the river, her unknown image became so fixed in his mind that he slept but little in the night, and having pulled on his clothes by break of day, crept tiptoeing past the nodding sentry at the gate, and, following the bend of the land, was not long of finding the river and the new-built tower.

But before ever he came in sight of the door so strangely set, there flashed, as it seemed, from the very wall of that stark prison a slender, white-clad shape, shooting outward and falling, with arms outstretched, headlong into the stream. Between the sinking and the rising again the watcher held his breath in fear. But when the head, wetted from brown gold almost to blackness, rose to the water's face, his dread was melted into admiration keen as the very pang of love; for the Princess, with never a backward glance, made straight for the island, swimming with grace and speed such as never before had he seen; so that, but for the dive and her white feet in the air, he had surely, he told himself, have taken her for some mermaid.

As she touched the shore of the island, the watcher hid himself among the willows of the bank, lest she should look behind her and see him. Then, loth to think that he might never see her again, the baron watched that island for many minutes after its feathery trees had hidden the delicate form which ran to shelter as surely as it had swum to safety; and after a while, round the upper point of the isle came dancing the tilted prow of a narrow boat—a little shallop fashioned from skins stretched upon a framework cunningly shaped and knit. And in its stern, clad in the wet garment which clung almost as it had been her skin, sat the Princess.

Unseen, he saw her land beneath the tower; saw her lift the two packets of clothes which she had dropped before diving, creep once more into her boat, and drive it again with firm strokes of her paddle to the island which this time hid her from his sight before she landed.

For a space he stood, his eyes empty, but his thought very full; then turned his face to the castle.

Three times before he came there he sighed; for now indeed was he truly in love.

The Princess, meanwhile, having clothed herself seemly on the sheltered shore of her refuge, made her way to the old fisherman's hut. When she had roused him from his slumber, he rose, rubbing sleep from eyes dazzled by the daylight and the lady's beauty.

They were old friends, this old man and the young Princess; for she owed him great part of her skill in matters concerning the water, so that her smile was his delight and her service his pleasure.

What she pleased, she told him, what she asked, he gave: his little boat, food to stock it, his old blessing upon her shining head, and the skill of his old hands to thrust her off from the shore on her wayward journey.

"Forty miles down stream," he said, before leaving his hold of the little craft, "where both banks are in the domain of the great King, you shall find an island such as this, but greater. 'Tis called *Brothers' Eyot*, because there dwell upon it two born at one birth, who are hunters and fishers—good men that you may trust!"

With that he pushed hard upon the boat, and as the water widened apace between them,

"There is no island between mine and theirs," he cried, and stood watching until even the little brown sail which the Princess had hoisted was too far down the long waters for his old eyes.

The sun being well risen, there came to the door of the tower a woman wrapped in a bedcover, and screaming. So, after a while, the old

Prince, with his guest and his guard, came riding over the meadows, with great hue and cry.

But in all that countryside there was but one did know which way the bird was flown, and one that guessed. But not from old fisher nor young noble did the Prince nor his company get any word.

Before that day was half spent, the baron rode on his way, having asked of the Prince (and bending down from his saddle to speak the more secretly):

"If I find her, sir, shall I have her?"

"Surely, my son," said the old man, speaking gentlier than his wont; "if you can also find a heart in her body."

Now, two days after this wonderful vanishing of the Princess from the tower, the elder of those twin brothers who dwelt upon the eyot over against the village which should first hear laughter, awoke a little after dawn, and went to the shelving beach to wash himself. When he had swum awhile, and the sweet water and sweeter air of the morning had cleared the sleep from his eyes, he espied a little shallop drifting unguided in the stream, and swam to it with purpose to fetch it ashore. But when, with a light hand on the prow, he had peered over the gunwale, he was smitten with great wonder and awe to see sleeping there soundly a lady more beautiful than he had thought could live.

Very gently he swam, and pushing her cradle out of the current, soon had it moored to a tree stump in the narrow bay that was their harbour and dock.

Still moving softly, he left the lady sleeping, and had scarce pulled on the clothes he had left lying on the beach, when his brother came to him. And even as he told of the wondrous thing he had found astray on the swift water, there arose a wish in him strange to his mind: for he was unwilling to lead his brother to the moored shallop, and was sad because the river islet was not all and solely his.

But when the brothers found the Princess awake, sitting up in her boat and binding the hair which had fallen about her, loose in splendour, the younger man's heart held the same desire and the same regret as the elder's. For they were born to think and to suffer alike, but not, for this time, as one.

So they led the lady to their house of two rooms; whence they carried each his private gear into the shed where they kept their fishing tackle, their bows and their spears, and tools for making and mending all that they needed. And the younger brother, that was the better hunter and trapper of beasts, took the smaller boat and went to the woods of the mainland to kill game for the lady's dinner. But the elder, that was the fisher, when he had hooked a fish or so, gave over his craft, and broiled his catch and milked his goat for her breakfast. And when she had eaten and would sleep again, having watched great part of her second night afloat, he took his heavy skiff across the stream to the village and there bought delicate food and good wine for his guest. And along with these he brought back to the island his sister also, who was married with a soldier away at the wars, that she might be companion and servant to the lady, whom thereafter they did all three for many days entertain with great honour; so that the brothers forgot all things (even to each other's love for that while) in worship of the fairest and most gracious mistress that the world could show; while the sister, loving the lady well also, yet marvelled at her brothers, and wondered grievously what should come of this. For the Princess, although she knew she could not stay in that eyot at hospitality for ever, yet was no day in the same mind for what must next he done.

Thus was the sister's fear the brothers' hope.

The Princess, inventing no way at all to depart with dignity, did, upon the seventh night, resolve her mind to steal away in the darkest hour of the eighth, down the great stream in her shallop, rather than further to burden the large charity of folk so poor.

But at noon of the eighth day comes a handsome boat, pulled up-stream by four skilled oarsmen. And the dwellers of the eyot stood watching this measured and stately approach, thinking that the fine barge with its carved, gilded and curtained shelter in the after-part, must soon pass them by, or turn aside for the harbour of the great village upon the shore. But straight for the island it came, nor slacked speed until half its keel was fast upon the shingle.

Then from the stern-house came forth a man, young, of good feature and grave bearing, and clad as in the country of our Princess the learned clerks and statesmen were habited, in cloth of sad colours, and very thoughtfully shaped.

And when the Princess saw him, her heart, though she knew not why, was afraid. And the brothers, with fierce bearing and a mind against his landing, came to the water's edge.

"Do you dwell here?" asked the stranger, standing in his boat.

"The eyot is ours, and all that is built and grows in it," said the elder brother, handling his angling pole as if it had been a soldier's pike.

"And who dwells here in your protection?" asked the stranger.

"Those whom I shall protect," replied the fisher, feeling a danger he knew not. "My brother and my sister."

"The lady behind you," said the stranger, "is not your sister."

So, with calm on her face and courage in her eye, the Princess came forward.

"I, sir, am a guest of these generous countrymen. And, since you do me the honour to know me, you will know that they have earned my father's thanks and your esteem, in sheltering me with such gentle observance."

Then the grave young man stepped ashore and stood uncovered before her, including in his reverent bearing her bodyguard that stood like hounds disappointed.

And the Princess said:

"But I think I do not know you, sir."

This was a true saying; for not then, nor until it was too late, did she even suspect that this grave, courteous man, in the semblance of an emissary, with pen in girdle, and the writer's wallet slung from it, was he from whom she had fled; having, indeed, drawn for herself a picture of some rude baron from the hills with more lands and flocks than good looks or gentle customs.

"I am a lawyer, Princess," he said, "that your father hath sent to parley with you."

And when he said *Princess*, the brothers looked at each other, and swiftly away. For each was wounded by that word, and looked, by habit, for the old kindness to ease his smart; and each drew his eyes away in a twinkling, for anger that his pain was also the other's.

"We have not broken fast, sir Lawyer," says the Princess. "Fisherman," she said, very graciously, "and huntsman, will you bid my naughty father's peace-herald to meat with us?"

So the fisherman bade him; but the huntsman, for the sorrow he had, could do no better than nod his head in agreement with his brother.

The boat with its crew being sent to the village to find food and quarters, with the order to return at such an hour, the sister and the two simple brothers set a very good meal before the Princess and the young noble that gave himself for nothing but a scribe.

Now, as they ate, the newcomer marked that the brothers scarce spoke with each other, nor exchanged even a glance of the eye in concord; of which strange matter he very soon suspected the reason. But the good sister was in hope that of a common enmity they should make a stepping-stone to reconciliation. So this honest woman, being after meat for a space alone with the Princess, asks of her did she know the cause which had brought anger between the brothers. The Princess, who gave again in full measure the love she had received from this gentle-hearted servant, was ashamed to answer, and said that she did not know why these men should not live in harmony. But an inkling she had, and wished herself well away from that island.

Thus it came that when the lady and the lawyer were left for their conference of state alone upon the greensward of an open space shaded by the fairest trees of the eyot, she was at first in a temper of mind very convenient for persuading.

"Your Highness's father," began the Prince's ambassador, "bids your return to him."

"Bids! Does he so?" cries the Princess. "Then should he come himself, with an army at his back."

For she neither liked this echo of commanding, nor was minded to show too docile all in a trice.

"He knows not by what road his daughter fled, nor whither to march his men," said the scribe.

"Yet have you found me, sir Lawyer," said the Princess.

"I have been taught," he replied, "to read much in small signs."

"What tracks did I leave for your scholarship?" she asked.

"I looked at that tower, Princess," he answered, "and I saw that its door was high enough for a skilful diver to reach the river in safety. The old gardener at your castle has told me that his Princess hath a bold spirit, being swift as a cat to scale a tree, swift as a bird to swoop from it into the lake (where in summer she will play the day long with her maidens), and in the water swifter than the fishes themselves."

"This is but guessing—an arrow sped at a venture, sir."

"There were others that hit the same mark. Upon the land side of the wall, madam, which keeps the river from the tower, is a patch of moist, sandy soil. And there I saw—I, and I only—the print of a slender and beautiful foot—two prints: the one naked and pointing with every sweet toe towards the tower, the other shod; and the shoe's heel was pressed deep, and was nearer to the tower than its tip."

The Princess wrinkled her brows in a frown of questioning.

"And from these?" she asked, "what knowledge do you read?"

"I read," said the scribe, his heart beating heavily in fear of the truth's leaking out, "that you had leapt headlong from the door to the river, had swum to the old fisherman's isle, returned in a boat, disembarked and fetched some matters which you had dropped to the tower's foot."

The face of the Princess was flushed like roses at sunrise.

"What matters do you read that I had left there?" she asked.

"What but your shoes, madam—of which you left me a clear sign in the wet sand. Shall I tell you the end of my reading?"

"No, sir Lawyer. One reads well, after the tale is told. I think the old fisherman has betrayed me."

"He told nothing, Princess. But you, by that very thought, tell me that my reading is true."

"Why, then," she asked, shifting her eyes from his, "did you not spell out this tale to my father? The faithful servant does not hide his knowledge to earn the higher reward."

"In this matter alone of finding your Highness am I his servant. I came to his castle in the cavalcade of the gentleman that should, I was told, espouse your Highness."

"Is it then that nobleman whom you serve?" she asked, and her eyes were now cold, and her mouth bent in scorn.

"At times, madam," answered the scribe, "I do serve him. But not always so well as he desires."

"Then you seek a better service, I must suppose?"

"I do," he said; and so looked upon her that she doubted both of his meaning and of her own uncouth disturbance of spirit.

She wished she were away, and therefore sat her down upon a felled tree that was near.

"And I thought," said the scribe, "that my learning in the art of persuasion might do more in reconcilement of your Highness and the Prince your father than all his stern commands and stiff men-at-arms. So I offered myself to bring you back, but would tell nothing of how nor whence; and the Prince gave me a writing."

The Princess, however, showed no care to read the parchment which he laid beside her.

"Now that you have found me," she said, "I pray you tell his daughter how you purpose fulfilling your mission?"

"If your Highness will show me," he replied, "the roots of the quarrel between you."

For a space she was silent and pensive; whereafter she raised her eyes and spoke to the young lawyer as to a judge accepted and worthy of her candour.

"Sir, he purposed selling me," she said, "to a certain nobleman that I knew not at all."

"*Selling* is a hard word," said the scribe. "In custom it is called giving."

"Call it as you will: it was to please himself, and, perhaps, this up-river yokel of a baron, sir, but with no thought to please me, that he was about making this marriage. So was I become a thing, a merchandise, a bale of goods; and since a man is not father to a farm, a war-horse nor a bag of corn, I said: 'I am free of governance,' and came here."

Ceasing, the Princess folded hands in lap, and looked upon the scribe with that woman's meekness which cries: "Touch me not?"

"And yet," he said foolishly, speaking without sense of his words, "— and yet you do belong to him."

"Belonging," quoth the Princess, "goeth hand in hand with loving. When I was very young, the Prince my father would let me love him— and did love me, I believe. But since I grew to this, he has forgotten. So have I my freedom, which I purpose keeping, loving it now of all things best."

"Had you but waited to see this suitor—" began the young man.

"I dared not," said the Princess.

"Did you fear his power more than your father's?"

"From him alone I feared nothing—scarce from him and my father together. But his suite—our household—my father's guard—all those eyes! A woman may give way to numbers—to the thousand fools, when she is as brass to the few, even though those few be wise. It was not safe, I said in my heart. With two hundred eyes of disfavour upon her, one might truckle for any shelter."

"I think you hold this suitor a boorish fellow," said the lawyer.

"I have not spoken with him, nor even seen him," she answered. "Tell me, you sir Lawyer, is he a fit mate for my station and my person?"

"Now that I have seen and spoken with you, Princess, I do not so think him. But a fit man were to seek. And esteem is so fickle in the granting, so various in cause, that you, should you meet this unmannered hedge-noble, might find him not wholly lacking in grace."

"I think," she replied, "that my divination and your judgment, sir Lawyer, would be little apart."

For a while they sat in silence, she with chin in palm, elbow on knee, thinking more of the scribe than of that baron; but he, more of the Princess than even of himself.

"You would take me back to my father," she resumed, "upon what terms?"

"Submission, madam," said the scribe, "to your duteous obedience."

The Princess rose from her seat.

"To-morrow," she said, "you shall help me to determine what obedience I owe, and to whom it is due."

So the Princess went into the hut of the fishermen, and the lover, forgetting baron and scribe, stood musing by the water until his barge fetched him away.

Within the hut was the soldier's wife.

"That is a fine and handsome young man," says she, when the Princess came to her.

"Is he so?" says she, very careless, "I did not mark it. The fellow is but a scribe, a mouthpiece, a go-between."

"When I saw him rise up in that fine barge of his," said the elder woman, "I did hope indeed it should be the lover whom you had never seen."

The Princess shook her head.

"That," she said, "were a matter very different."

And the soldier's wife, for all her thought upon it, did not ask what this difference might be, between the man she had not marked and another whom she had not seen.

But the Princess fell into a silence, which held her until the return of her father's messenger.

Now, in this second meeting, which should have been a solemn parley concerning the daughter's surrender to her father, the scribe and the lady held converse for many hours, and spoke of all things save that for which they were met; so that they parted at sundown with no end in the matter reached.

"To-morrow," she said, "I will tell you my fixed purpose."

For a matter so grave the scribe thought well to come before the time set. Yet was the Princess ready, waiting upon his coming.

No sooner was he risen from his knee and the kissing of her hand, than she spoke of the matter which the day before they had neglected.

"My mind," she said, "is set at last. Never will I go back to wed, nor ever to encounter that—how was it you named him?—that up-river yokel. I am done with him."

"Done with him," said the scribe, "before ever you did begin."

"Ay!" said the Princess, and nodded her head as setting a term to the matter.

"You would not go, I think," said her lover, "to marry any man."

"None of my father's choice," answered the Princess.

The young man looked into her eyes and twice ere he spoke breathed deeply.

"What if the choosing were mine?" he asked.

"I would consider of it," said the Princess.

"You would trust me?" he asked again.

"So far as listen to your reasons, sir Lawyer. For I think you are wise. Have you a suitor in mind?"

"I have. But I can plead no case for him, nor no merit save one."

"One is enough, if it be the right merit."

"A merit which is none; for he cannot help but love you, Princess. Will you embark and go with me—to stay with me always?"

Then the Princess bent on him a gaze of so high yet so tender a courage that soon he spoke again.

"Wilt thou take ship with me, lady?" he asked, beseeching.

"With you, sir," she answered, "in any ship, for what harbour you please. But with no other man, nor for no other, will I budge one yard from the kind safety of this eyot."

So for that day until the sun was down, and the next, the long day through, these lovers forgot father and baron, duty and danger, in the beauty which, like an aureate fog, wrapped them together, while yet it sundered them from even their small world of that island.

74

But this division was theirs alone: for huntsman and fisher knew what they saw; so that, his own cripple-born hope being dead, each, in his unreason of jealous passion, was nigh ready to slay his brother.

Their sister, seeing how it stood with them, was yet glad that this other woman, whom she had succoured, should have her bosom filled with a joy more lovely even than her face; and thought within herself: "This will take her hence, whereafter I shall know her no more. Yet, she being gone, I shall deal wisely with these brethren of mine, that begin to hate each other for the brightness of the moon which neither may reach."

Now the scribe had bidden them all to a feast for that last night; and the brothers, that had given so freely, could not deny him on their own land. A table, therefore, with fine food and good wine from the village, was dressed in the glade which the Princess loved; and this company of five sat down to supper as the moon rose, shining level down the breast of the river upon all their faces.

And when they had eaten for a while and drunk a little, the host of the feast told them, with a pleasant modesty, how he and the Princess should next morning be married before the headman of the village, and thereafter set forth afloat upon their wedding journey.

And though the women, peasant and princess, saw dark looks on the faces of fisherman and hunter, the giver of the feast saw nothing, but believed in that moment all men as joyful as he, and made thanks to these two and the soldier's wife for the good service rendered to his lady in her need.

Eating and drinking being at an end, the Princess yet stood awhile, looking upon the water and the climbing moon, holding her lover's arm and talking with him. And the three other guests, standing silent apart, could not but hear some words of what was spoken between them.

"If you take me up stream, beloved, and back to my father," said the Princess, "I shall hold you the bravest man in all the world."

"Art afeared thyself, Princess?" asked her lover.

"Of nothing that lives, if you be with me," she answered. "But what should I fear, sweet lady? Did I not say I would fetch his daughter to him, and shall I not do this?"

"You will take him a daughter not only unwilling but unable, sir Lawyer, to obey him in the matter of our quarrel."

"If we be husband and wife when we appear before him," said the scribe, "he is already obeyed."

The Princess drew herself away from him, yet keeping her hold of his arm.

"I do not understand," she said.

"Beloved," he replied, "have you never guessed that I am that suitor from whom you fled?"

Then a black speck that there was in the heart of the Princess so swelled and spread itself, that in a moment she was filled with the darkness, and could not speak.

"From the beginning," he went on, "I had in mind to tell you this before we should be wed. But since that yesterday my lips met with yours, I have forgot all things save our love and your beauty. For sure, you will not fall to hating your hedge-baron once more for the being less odious than your conceit of him."

But now the blackness in her heart was turned to fire of anger, burning red.

"Were I a man," she cried, "I would slay you." And her hand pushed from her the arm to which it had clung.

"To steal my love by subtle pretences, that you might lead me, meekly following, before my father, showing him how craftier is thy treachery than his rude cruelty—that is a crime of the lickspittle courtier, a coveter of lands, offices and princely favour."

And the fire grew within her ever hotter towards the white heat of hate; so that, with every first word that her lover would speak, the scalding torrent of her invective words would whelm him afresh, all her speech being sharply heard even by the two brothers and their sister standing astonished.

At last the fisher, in a whispering voice, gave his censure that truly this lawyer fellow had bitterly wronged their lady.

But the huntsman, for all that his worship of the Princess inclined him to be of her part in the quarrel, could not in that moment be in any agreement with the brother whose love he had foregone for jealousy. Wherefore:

"Not so," he said. "For he has but taken a shrewd way to plumb the little depth of the lady's love; by which I, for my part, am very well pleased."

His voice was raised above his brother's, and their sister perceived that the storm which had been brewing between them was about bursting in thunder; so that she seized them by each an arm and forced them to go with her behind the hut.

"Here," she said, "you may quarrel like fools, and fight, if you must, like evil men. But our lady shall have privacy for her anger and her grief."

" 'Tis her pride is hurt," quoth the younger brother.

"The lie in thy teeth!" cries the elder. "It is her love betrayed," and smote his brother on the mouth.

Now as these two fell a-fighting with hands in place of words, a wave of the Princess's anger did leave behind it a hollow of exhaustion so wide and deep that her lover found space for speech.

"I perceive," he said (and in his heart also there was now anger, yet not in his voice)" —I perceive that the great love of which you have told me is a small thing beside your childish pride of prevailing over an old man foolishly incensed."

And because she would not confess the truth of his saying, yet knew it, her anger revived, and she drew near him with gnashing teeth and eyes bright with a rage of scorn.

"I would you had died ere you found me," she said. "If hatred could kill—"

"It cannot," said the baron, "but a knife may, fitly handled." And so gave her the poniard from his girdle, and stood before her, hands falling to his sides. And she took the knife, seeking in herself for the courage and cruelty to use it.

But there came even then to the island, rippling and tinkling over the moonlit water, the first note of the Elf's first laughing.

The unhappy lover heard it, and knew that a strange ally had joined in his battle; but the joy of the thing itself came not yet into his heart. For the joy that he sought must come from his lady's face, which he read with burning eyes and a vast aching in his breast.

In the beginning, as it seemed, the Princess forgot all things—her spite of anger, her lover, the moon above and the grass under her feet; forgot even herself in the trickling of that sacred merriment by the funnel of her ear into the vessel of her heart. Her white arms fell to her sides, the dagger lay and shone among the grass-blades, and she flung back her head so that her lover saw the fair throat lift and tremble with laughter which might not at first come out. When come it did, the man who watched and listened found this newer music stranger and more thrilling than even that which, having fathered it, still came pealing to them over the water in concert with its human offspring; so that, to this lover's mind, until he came to die, the first and the most merry laughter was ever hers whom he loved.

But when she had laughed with a full throat and a passion growing until the breath left her body faster than she might fetch it back, and the indrawn gaspings divided the joyous chain with jarring links, fear took him and he laid a hand upon her.

At the touch, her chin came slowly downward, and the laughter bubbled softer through its gateway of shining teeth and lips subtly bending to new shapes. And then her eyes looked into his, and he found love in them.

But in his the woman found memory of how she had used him; and in his face all the goodness and beauty which had so little deserved this usage.

Then came her laughing to an end, and she fell at his feet, and was covered with shame, as with a cloak that is no shield.

Now the Princess was not the first to laugh upon the Brothers' Eyot; for on the hut's other side was one that had no thought of herself that night, and in her heart no pain save the longing to which she was well used. Her brothers' fighting, she thought, might well be the quick road to revision of love; and, left to herself, why should not the Princess (thought the soldier's wife) find the humble road back to her joy?

So, when the elfin notes reached her, they touched her heart at once to unknown mirth, which flowed from her again in a happy chuckling, too soft to reach the Princess and her lover. But the brothers heard her, and, after her, the laughing Elf; whereupon, giving over their fighting, they came to their sister, and, seeing at last clearly the merriment in her loving eyes and enraptured lips, they could by no means ask her of it before falling themselves into a like but louder response. And in that very moment they heard the royal laughter of the Princess rising clear among the trees beyond their house.

Then the brothers would have run to see how she fared; but the sister bade wait awhile.

The laughter of the Princess broke of a sudden and ceased, even before the last sweet note of the Elf died upon the air.

When all was silent, the fisher asked of his sister, what was it they had heard and themselves repeated. But she smiled and shook her head.

" 'Tis a good thing, at any reading," said the huntsman, with an arm about his brother's shoulder; "for it hath made a fool know his folly."

"Two fools," said the fisherman, "if you be one."

So they went, after a while, to the Princess, and offered her service, and she bade them come with her upon her wedding journey.

On the morrow, when the headman had married the Baron to the Princess, the fine barge had six rowers instead of four. But the sister of two stood on the quay calling good luck upon them, and went home smiling to wait for her soldier.

Now, in the heat of the day, when their boat lay cool beneath hanging willows, many a mile upstream, the lovers sent their crew ashore for a space, and talked much together of their love, and of the life they should spend in company.

And after a while the Baron told his Princess more of his first falling in love with her. But, before he was gone far with his tale:

"Why, then," she cries, breaking in upon it, "you must needs have seen my leap from the tower."

"In mid air—like a swallow swooping—that was my first vision," he replied. And the Princess tried to cover all the redness of her cheeks with white fingers.

"Nay, prithee, do not!" he said. "I did not look for you. But you flashed upon me out of a prison."

"Oh, but I blush, sir," she said, "for that shift—a garment very ill fashioned, that I stole from my serving woman. My own was a worthier, but safe and dry in my packet at the tower's foot."

"Poor serving-maid" said the husband, and told her of the woman wrapped in a bed-cover, and screaming from the high door of the tower.

Whereat the Princess laughed until the breath was nigh out of her.

"Princess," said the bridegroom, when she was silent and he had watched her awhile in that green shadow, "if ever I be sick or sorry wilt thou laugh to me?"

"Truly will I," she answered him. "And thou: if ever again in wicked passion I misuse or miscall thee, do thou laugh to me as that spirit did laugh to us all, last night across the water."

When at last they stood before the old Prince:

"I have kept my word, Highness," says the Baron.

" 'Tis well," replied the bride's father, very close and grim of face. "And now, willy, nilly, she shall marry you."

His daughter then showing him the first smile that ever he had seen, the old man wondered what ailed her: yet thought it was neither pride nor sickness.

"Willy, nilly, sir," she said, "marry the gentleman is what I cannot do. For I am already these three days his wife."

Then the old Prince, what with his long waiting and his love soured in anger, waxed exceeding wroth when they told him their story; for he saw his vengeance taken from him.

But the Princess said:

"That a man should get his desire, and then cry out upon them that bring it to him, is truly a matter for laughter."

"Laughter? Laughter!" cries the Prince; for the word was newer yet to him than to her that had made it. "What is laughter?"

"Why, this!" said his daughter: and laughed as she had laughed in the moonlight on the Brothers' Eyot.

Then her lover and his boat's crew took up the tune, and the bodyguard and all the princely household joined them in it, until the master of them broke from anger into a great shout of such merriment as left him mighty clement, and, for that time, well nigh young again.

# X

## Joy and the Builder

In that same village dwelt a man that was a builder—the same that one day should build the fair house which arose behind the Gates of Welcome.

And because he thought much upon his work, and, indeed, would often dream the night through among visions of palaces, homesteads, castles and cottages, surpassing all that his bodily eye had seen for beauty conjoined with fitness, his spirit was sometimes sad with knowing that, of the few men in those parts who had need of a new house, there was none that truly understood convenience nor loved beauty.

He had even dreamed, in those later days before the Elf came, of one that had come to him, saying: "Build me a house." And this dream, often though he would dream it, could never go further; for with the joy of the command came ever the end of sleep, leaving him with the pale daylight shining upon the two temples of the village, and a day's work of controlling his craftsmen that mended some barn, or dug foundations for some ugly dwelling.

Now, of those two temples which he saw every day from his window, the one was built heavily of great stone blocks, very square and hopeless to look upon, having a door midway of each side, and square windows above. And within was an altar at each corner of the square floor, so that no worshipper looked in the face of another.

But the second was a great gilded fane, like a globe sunken halfway into the earth. There were many windows, like sleepy eyes, and but two doors in all its single wall; the one for entrance, narrow to the bare width of a man's shoulders, and the other for going out, whence four might come abreast. Herewithin was an altar in the floor's middle, the very centre of ring beyond ring of curved benches, to seat a multitude of which each man might see the face of every other.

And the builder knew the creed of each temple as well as he could have limned on his tablet the shape of the building which housed it.

For in the earliest days which he could recall, his mother would take him on the middle day of the week to the round, yellow-shining temple where the congregation adored an effigy of its own qualities, calling this image MAN, and where the faithful spoke of themselves as WE, and of their gathering place as The House of US.

81

Again, from his tenth year, his father would take him, upon the last day of each week, to the square temple where, in short invocations divided by long silences, men worshipped a force which could help neither them nor itself; a power of which, indeed, they knew so little that it was named among them IT—IT Inevitable and Supreme.

And recalling each parent's solemn observance of religion, he would wonder now in manhood that they had never found in their difference of belief cause of dispute nor any unhappiness. But he would remember further how he had asked his father who was it did send the rain upon the earth.

"Do we not," his father had answered, "say always: IT raineth, IT bloweth, IT sendeth the heat and the cold?"

"And what," asked the child, "is IT?"

"Who knoweth?" said the man.

But the boy persisted.

"IT! Is IT good? Is IT bad? Is IT like unto us, my father?"

" 'Tis taught in the temple, my son, that in no wise is IT like unto us; and therefore is our measuring of good and evil altogether strange unto IT."

"Shall I know more of it, when I am grown to a man?" asked the son.

"Because we cannot see IT, my son, we call IT blind; nor hear IT, therefore deaf. IT is and IT must be, but without knowledge we worship."

Silenced, yet in no wise answered, the boy, coming three days thereafter from the gilded dome with his mother, had plied her in turn with childish inquiries. And when she had told him in terms lame rather than simple her temple's easy doctrine of a single, widespread spirit of MAN, immanent in all things and all men, he must ask again: "Is that Spirit good?"

"There are good men, and good women and good children, like thee, my son," she replied. "Therefore must the Spirit of MAN be a good spirit."

"There be bad men also, my mother," began the boy; but when he saw a frowning of pain on her forehead, he kept the conclusion of his reasoning within his own mind.

It was, indeed, but this: that his father's IT was a thing little adorable, since was found therein no knowledge and no goodness; and that the spirit to which his mother bowed was mixed of good and evil, so that a child might not, for any light her temple could let shine, discover difference between the bad thing and the good.

Man-grown and orphaned, he would, in brooding upon the unshapen desire that he had, make argument with himself of his father's seeking closeness to the hearts of his kind in the bond of their common fate, while his mother sought assuagement of the common suffering in community of resistance or palliation.

Some little pleasure each had indeed taken from life; much, he knew, they had given to their son; for they, being gone, yet showed him by their absence what, even so, men and women may be to one another. And yet this measuring of his loss taught him further that the thing unnamed, after which, boy and man, he longed, was above and beyond all that they had to give.

For even in those days there was found, here and there among men, one that held in his dim soul knowledge of a need, a lacking; a thirst, as it were, after a liquid of which the golden radiance and immortal impulse were yet perceived but as the sun's light through the sealed eyelids of some new-born puppy.

Just so the builder knew not what he sought, but knew very surely that always was he seeking. For not yet had the Elf looked upon the meeting of Joy with Sorrow on the hillside, between moorland and forest.

Yet there grew stronger in him belief that this thirst which he had was the need of the temple which was square, as of that which was round; and that, unless he should find what he fumbled for, seeking without direction, he would never see, even in his dream, the beauty of the house which in that dream he had been commanded to build.

Three times in the years since he was alone had he said, to himself: "At last I have found it." And each time that which he had found died in his fingers; and of each dead thing he said as he laid it aside: "This thing was a good thing, but still do I seek."

Then there came a day when the man's spirit lay exceeding heavy in his breast; and it was the same day upon which, in the last hour, the Elf should laugh.

And the builder stirred himself, and said: "I will draw shapes and plans of houses until I be weary. And perchance I shall find among them a form which shall tell me what I know not."

Until it was night, so that at last he must work by light of candle, did he draw and plan, measuring and shaping such castles and temples, houses and workshops as he wished that men would command of him. So that in the end he was weary indeed, and a voice cried within his darkened heart: "In what are these better than those which they have?"

Of which weariness and lowness of spirit, as the moon was rising, the builder fell asleep, with his arms for pillow betwixt head and table.

Through the walls of his slumber there came to him music, which was the laughing of the Elf upon the village green. And once more his dream was upon him, of the command that was given: "Build for me a house!"

And the music, which was laughter leaking through to the chamber of his dream, did so interpret and make plain to him that command (which came to him from lips which he could not see) that he knew in that very stroke of time what manner of house he must build for the dwelling place of him that so commanded.

Then he opened his eyes, and looked from his window, and saw once more the two temples clear in the moonlight. Knowing not nor heeding the newness of his own utterance, he laughed in his throat at the gilded roundness, and,

" 'Tis thrust up through the earth, and sticketh half-way," he said; but of the other temple, with its low, thick walls like patient shoulders of stone; "It is pushed down into earth, but is yet too strong for burial complete."

Then having tasted his own laughter once more,

"But Joy's Temple," he cried (having perceived in the very finding of his treasure the name that was written there) "—but Joy's Temple shall soar like a flame drawn upward and leaping for ever."

Whereafter, in the growing light of his new day, he fell a-working with his pencils and rulers and compasses upon the first planning and picturing of that house which so often he had been commanded to conceive and to build. And now, while the scheme of beauty was shed from him in crowding conceits of delight to take form upon his parchment, he was so little weary that he doubted whether he were awake or in the second chapter of his old dream. But awaking from slumber wholly dreamless, when the sun was past its height, and fearing that all his joy and labour were lost in that house of broken pledges, the builder laughed aloud with great comfort to find his accomplished work lying about him in sheet upon sheet of finished design. And when he had examined them in order, he knew that no dream was so good as this work of his.

For he had conceived the Temple of Joy which should arise from mighty foundations in walls and columns of stone, stronger than fate, more lovely than any temple of man. Seen from afar, it should reach upward with great arms dwindling in ascent to slender fingers of undeviating aspiration, clear-stamped upon their background of light, whether grey cloud, azure of summer noon, or deep, star-jewelled blue of midnight. Drawn nearer, you should see a fair pattern in stone, light as foliage, strong as steel; the strength of arched window and door, the loving weight and deft angle of buttress and keystone; and ever as the eye went upward, a window lighter and more up-reaching than the last.

But, come so near that his eyes might embrace in a glance barely the width of two windows, a man should begin, perhaps, to read the story written in the stones of these walls; yet not until he had there spent the leisure of half a lifetime should he come at an end of that book.

For by the carver's chisel should be wrought into this great upheaval every pleasure and every pain, every error and every making straight, all truth in myth and every falsehood of history, the small sin, the great sacrifice, tales of witch, goblin, and fairy, the record of brave battles and cruel defeat, of victory and renunciation, of oppression suffered and freedom won, to warm a man's heart with his father's memories, and to show him, if he would see them, the hands drawn upward out of this medley of his passion, in search of the new thing which should bring harmony into the jangling, and lovely reason into the broken tale of a fool.

Some say that before he died the builder saw in very stone his Temple of Joy; others, that he died in great content, having found that for which he left the great shrine well begun.

But all agree that over his tomb were carved these words of his making:

> "Who seeketh pleasure eateth burnt bread.
> Who findeth Joy hath all pleasure in his pocket."

The Books of Ronald MacDonald (1860-1933)

*The Sword of the King*
    London: John Murray, [May] 1900
    New York: The Century Co., 1900

*God Save the King*
    London: Hutchinson & Co., [November] 1901
    New York: The Century Co., 1901

*Camilla Faversham*
    London: Hutchinson & Co., [October] 1903

*The Sea Maid*
    London: Methuen & Co., [February] 1906
    New York: Henry Holt, 1906

*A Human Trinity*
    London: Methuen & Co., [March] 1907

*The Election of Isabel*
    London: Edward Arnold, [October] 1907

*The Carcase*
    London: Everett & Co., [November 1909]

*The Red Herring*
    London: Everett & Co., [July] 1910

*The First of the Ebb*
    London: Everett & Co., [February] 1911
    Everett's Library [August] 1912

"George MacDonald: A Personal Note"
    in *From a Northern Window*
            London: Nisbet, [March] 1911

*Raymond Lanchester*
    London: John Murray, [November] 1912
    New York: John Lane Company, 1913 [as: *Lanchester of Brasenose*]

*Gambier's Advocate*
    London: Everett & Co., [June 1914]
    New York: John Lane Company, 1914

*Ambrotox and Limping Dick*, as by Oliver Fleming [co-authored with Philip MacDonald]
    London: Ward, Lock & Co., [July] 1920

*The Green Handkerchief*
    London: Cecil Palmer, [September 1922]

*The Laughing Elf*
    Oxford: Basil Blackwell, [November] 1922 [Illus. by Roy Meldrum]
    London: Cecil Palmer, 1932 [second edition]

*The Spandau Quid*, as by Oliver Fleming [co-authored with Philip MacDonald]
    London: Cecil Palmer, [April] 1923

Also published by Nodens Books


*Above Ker-Is and Other Stories*, by Evangeline Walton

This volume collects Evangeline Walton's ten completed fantasy short stories, including her 1950 story published in the legendary magazine *Weird Tales*, and three superb Breton tales which first appeared in anthologies in the early 1980s. Four stories are published here for the first time.

"Most of Walton's short stories are, like her novels, seamless blends of history, myth, and local color. . . . Walton's renown as a lyrical fantasist nothwithstanding, her short stories reveal that she had quite a flare for horror. . . . This slim, thoughtfully organized book is a wonderful addition to Walton's bibliography, and it gives readers a taste of what she might have achieved had she stuck to the short fiction path."

*Locus Magazine*

Also published by Nodens Books

*Lady Stanhope's Manuscript and Other Stories*, by Dale Nelson

*Lady Stanhope's Manuscript and Other Stories* collects eleven stories written and published over the last thirty years. Some are written in the tradition of the antiquarian ghost story as established by M.R. James. Others may perhaps be classified as "strange stories" in the mode of Robert Aickman.

Dale Nelson's stories have appeared in *Ghosts and Scholars*, *Fungi*, and books from Ash-Tree Press and Tartarus Press. His articles have appeared in *Tolkien Studies*, *Lovecraft Studies*, *Studies in Weird Fiction*, *Mythlore*, Mallorn, and *Fadeaway*, and he is a columnist for the Tolkien newsletter *Beyond Bree* and *CSL: The Journal of the New York C. S. Lewis Society*.

Also published by Nodens Books

Nodens Chapbooks:

*Sable Revery: Poems, Sketches, Letters*, by Robert Nelson

*The Ghost in the Tower: Sketches of Lost Jacobia*, by Earl H.
    Reed

*The Man Who Lived Backwards and Other Stories*, by Charles
    F. Hall

Made in the USA
Middletown, DE
24 September 2017